For Gavin,

Family is the ~~xero~~ source of power. Always look after your family and you will never lose your power!

Michell Plested

Mik Murdoch:

The Power Within

Michell Plested

FIVE RIVERS PUBLISHING
WWW.FIVERIVERSPUBLISHING.COM

Published by Five Rivers Publishing, 704 Queen Street, P.O. Box 293, Neustadt, ON N0G 2M0, Canada

www.fiveriverspublishing.com

Edited by Lorina Stephens

Interior design and layout by Lorina Stephens

Title set in 123 Marker, designed by Oliver Mordefroid at www.123dev.net

Byline set in Arial Rounded MT Bold by Microsoft

Body set in Garamond designed by Tony Stann for the International Typeface Croporation, influenced by the 16th century serif typefaces attributed to punch-cutter Claude Garamont.

Publisher's note: This book is a work of fiction. Names, characters, places and incidents either are the products of the author's imagination or are used fictitiously, and any resemblance to actual persons living or dead, events, or locales is entirely coincidental.

Published in Canada

Library and Archives Canada Cataloguing in Publication

Plested, Michell, 1968-, author

Mik Murdoch : the power within / Michell Plested.

Issued in print and electronic formats.

ISBN 978-1-927400-67-8 (pbk.).—ISBN 978-1-927400-68-5 (epub)

I. Title.

PS8631.L47M56 2014   jC813'.6   C2014-903675-2

C2014-903676-0

For all those people who have supported me with *Mik Murdoch: Boy Superhero* and especially to Tigana Runté who told her dad Mik was worth publishing in the first place.

Contents

Chapter 1

Waiting is hard. Really, really hard! Especially when the thing you are waiting for is the one thing you want most in the world.

In my case, the one thing I want most is a super power. Not your everyday dream.

And who am I? I'm Mik Murdoch, and I'm a super hero.

It may sound strange to call myself a super hero when I don't have any powers, but you don't need to have superhuman abilities to be a hero. For example, I've battled turkey men, defeated Candy Bandits and even helped find the Cave of Wonders.

And it won't be long now before I do have a power.

You see, several months ago, on my birthday, I was given a magical berry that will give me super powers. I know this because the berry was given to me by the guardian from the Cave of Wonders. The same guardian who gave my friend, Miss Purdy, a piece of fruit that gave her some amazing powers of her own.

I've waited this long to eat the berry because I wanted to be sure of the power I would get. Okay, maybe I don't know what power I will get, but I figured giving it some thought wouldn't hurt and it would be better learning how to use my new power in the summer when school is out.

School! Wouldn't it be amazing to have my new abilities before school is over? I could try to help out my fellow students if they had a problem.

That thought made up my mind.

I opened my nightstand drawer and carefully dug down to the bottom. It would never do to leave the berry right at the top because occasionally my mom came up to clean up my room. Usually that happened after I forgot to do it myself a few times. Her cleaning sometimes included grabbing what she considered to be junk from inside my nightstand.

My fingers closed around the metal Altoid tin I used to store the berry in and I pulled it out of the drawer.

My hands were trembling a little as I opened the tin. Inside, wrapped in a clean paper towel, was the berry. I set the paper towel on my bed and unfolded it. I hadn't looked at the berry in a while (it was too tempting) and I half-expected it to be dried up.

It wasn't. It still looked like it had just been picked.

I guess I shouldn't have been surprised. It was magical, after all.

I picked it up off the towel, studying it, wondering at how plump and fresh it still looked. A small whine of concern broke my concentration.

The whining came from my best friend in the world and trusted sidekick, my dog Krypto.

I scratched behind his ears with my free hand. "What do

you think, Krypto? Should I finally eat this berry or should I wait a bit longer?"

Krypto is pretty smart and there are many times when I am sure he understands me. Too bad he can't talk. I looked down at the berry, puzzling over what to do.

Krypto padded over to me and nosed the berry toward me.

For a second I was afraid he might breathe it in. I mean, it would be cool to have a super powered pal, but I really wanted powers of my own.

He didn't though and I picked the berry up to look more closely at it.

Krypto cocked his head to the side and gave a little yip of encouragement. He nuzzled my arm, looking at me with his big brown eyes.

Krypto has never led me astray, so before I could talk myself out of it, I popped the berry into my mouth.

I crunched down on the berry and it burst, flooding my mouth with sweetness. I wasn't sure if I should just swallow it or if I should chew it for a while to get the most out of it.

In the end I decided to chew on it for a while, going so far as to keep a small amount under my tongue for luck. I sat down and scratched behind Krypto's ears while I chewed. He put his head on my knees and closed his eyes. Whenever I stopped scratching, he nosed my hand again to encourage me to continue.

When I swallowed the last bit of it, I waited. Quite honestly, I wasn't sure what to expect. When Miss Purdy ate her fruit, she got her powers almost immediately. This being a berry instead of something bigger, maybe it would take longer.

The more I waited, the more I thought about what I'd just done. How crazy was I? I mean, what would Mom say if I suddenly burst into flame or I grew huge muscles? Being in the house, I wouldn't have a hope of hiding that.

The treehouse! That would be safer! I raced down the stairs, Krypto chasing me all the way. I wasn't moving any faster than normal so I guessed that the new ability probably wasn't super-speed.

Mom asked as we hurtled by: "Where are you off to in such a hurry?"

"Just going out to the treehouse, Mom," I yelled as I passed. The windows didn't explode, so super-yelling couldn't be the power. "Krypto and I have a few things to do."

"Have fun! Back by suppertime! Please?"

"Yup!" I couldn't help but notice, as I slammed out of the door, Mom seemed relieved to have me out of the house.

I shook my head. I was probably just imagining things.

I ran all the way to the treehouse, slowing a little as I went by the garage where I could hear the radio playing. Dad must be out there tinkering on something again. From the volume of the music, I was sure he was having a nice time of it. I could almost feel the happiness radiating from the shop.

The steers all looked up at us with their big brown eyes as we ran past. They seemed content, if a little bored.

Krypto barked at the steers, but, aside from a couple lowering their heads at him, they watched us pass. That was the game they played. Krypto acted like the boss and they ignored him. At least, when I was around. I don't actually know if Krypto goes into the pasture alone.

The few times strangers came into the field, the steers weren't quite so calm. Like the time I had been attacked in my treehouse by the turkey men. The mooing and carrying on by the steers was so loud, the police came to investigate.

I scrambled up the treehouse ladder and Krypto ran up the ramp Dad and I had built for him, and finally we were safe from prying eyes. Nothing to do but wait for my new powers to appear. Have I said how hard waiting is?

I looked around the treehouse and realized just how long it had been since we last spent time in it. It must have been months because leaves and litter were all over. My stack of research material was all over the floor. I knew I hadn't left things that way, but the winter winds had been pretty strong. The tree does sway in the wind and breezes can creep in through the shuttered windows and through Krypto's ramp so that might have been why there was a mess.

I sighed when I looked around, dismayed by the piles of leaves and the clumps of flies. Might as well clean up while I waited. I knelt down on the floor and started by picking up issues of Iron Man, Spider-man and The Batman, careful not to misplace the scraps of paper that saved important reference pages. Krypto brought me a couple issues that had blown to the far side of the treehouse.

"Thanks, buddy," I said, scratching at his ears. Krypto leaned into my fingers and let out a sigh. I'm not sure what it is with dogs and itchy places, but no matter how long I scratch, he doesn't get tired of the attention.

I grabbed the broom to start sweeping and Krypto cleared leaves from his bowl by tipping it over and then nosing it out of the way.

You see how well we know each other?

With Krypto helping, I started to clean for real. I straightened out the comic books and swept all the dirt and debris out. Krypto moved the smaller items out of the way with his nose and mouth as I swept. I climbed up onto the observation deck on the roof and checked everything for loose boards. There were a couple and I made a mental note to borrow Dad's hammer to fix that problem next time I came out. I certainly didn't want to have someone lean on the rail only to fall to the ground!

I checked all the weapons next. The cow pie launchers were fine, but the arsenal of ammunition was dried out. The cow pies themselves would still make fine Frisbees but they wouldn't stop any attackers. I would have to collect more to keep my defensive weapons ready. The barrel of water for my super soakers was full and the water guns were in good working order. Water wouldn't scare anyone off, but it was good to have that much available.

We worked hard and by the time the treehouse was clean, I realized several hours had passed. Several hours and there were still no signs of any super powers.

What could be taking the powers so long?

Krypto lay down in his dog basket to have a snooze. He made the occasional whimper and bark in his sleep.

At least one of us was having a good time.

Then it occurred to me that maybe something about my body had changed. Something I might not have noticed.

I pulled off my shirt and pants. No new muscles, wings, gills or anything else out of the ordinary.

I shook my head. This was getting frustrating. I got dressed and climbed back up on the roof of the treehouse and lay on my back to stare at the sky through the tree's branches. I could still see my launching platform above me. I would have to check it out too to make sure no loose pieces were on it.

That wasn't my problem right now.

Something tickled in the back of my brain. Krypto was awake and someone was coming to the treehouse. Since the cattle weren't getting excited, it had to be either my mom or my dad.

I climbed off the roof of the treehouse just as I heard the creaking of the ladder. Someone was coming up. Moments later, Dad's head popped through the hatch.

"Hey, Mik. Your mom said you were in here." He looked around. "Your treehouse is looking good. I'm glad to see it survived the winter."

"Hi, Dad. Krypto and I came up to check everything. I decided to do a little cleaning while I was here."

Dad nodded. "Always a good idea. Keep things tidy and fixed up and they will never let you down."

"Somebody told me that once," I said with a smile, and watched his face as he recognized the fact I did listen to the advice he scattered in our conversations. "Ship-shape, is what it's called I think."

"Ship-shape," he agreed, laughing at my mimicry of one of his favourite phrases. "Anything need fixing up here?" Dad asked, pulling himself up through the hatch into the treehouse.

"I've got a couple loose boards on the upper railing," I said. "I thought I would borrow a hammer to fix them, if that's okay."

"I thought there might be." He held up a hammer and an old paint pail. "I brought you some supplies. The hammer is yours if you want it and I put some nails, screws and a multi-head screwdriver in the pail. Should be enough to keep you going for a while."

Wow! Some tools of my own. "Thanks Dad! That's great." I took the offered tools from him and set them on a crate I had sitting in the corner. "I'll get right to work."

"Well, you might have to wait a little while to break those tools in," Dad said with a smile. "Your mom actually sent me over to collect you for supper."

Supper? "Is it supper time already?" I asked. "I guess I completely lost track of the time."

"Close enough to supper, Mik." Dad made a 'come with me' gesture with his head. "Let's go wash up. I think your mom cooked a roast for us tonight. I don't know about you, but I'm starving." Dad started back down the ladder.

"Come on, Krypto. Time for supper," I said. I wandered over to the hatch and started to climb down. Krypto jumped to his feet and ran to his ramp. I could hear his toenails skittering across the floor of the treehouse as I closed the hatch and made my way down the ladder.

Then I remembered. The powers! A feeling of disappointment swept through me and I stopped my descent. Had I waited too long? Did all of the magic leech out of the berry and it was only ordinary when I finally ate it?

"You coming, Mik?" my father called from below. I could feel his eagerness to get back to the house.

"Coming, Dad," I said. I had to believe that the berry worked and I just didn't know what the power was yet. Maybe I could see in the dark or have laser vision and I just didn't know it yet.

Whatever it was, I had to keep my hopes up. To come so close and fail to get super powers would be more than I could bear.

Chapter 2

Krypto and I had supper with Mom and Dad. The food was as good as always; Mom is a terrific cook. I just couldn't enjoy it because thoughts of the wayward super powers kept intruding on my thoughts.

"You okay, Mik?" Mom asked me on more than one occasion.

"I'm fine, Mom. Just thinking about the work I need to do on the treehouse," I replied.

She laughed at that. "Good thing tomorrow is Sunday, then. You can spend all day working in your treehouse." She gave me a warning look. "That is, if all of your homework is done."

"No homework, Mom," I replied. "The teachers don't give homework in the last two weeks of school."

"Is that all there is left?" Dad asked. "Huh, time flies when you're having fun, doesn't it?"

I wasn't quite sure what Dad was talking about. Sure I liked school, but there were days I wouldn't say that going to school is the same as having fun. If I had the choice I would much rather be out exploring with Krypto. I decided to humour him. "Sure, Dad. Whatever you say."

Dad laughed. "Well, enjoy the last few days, buddy. You will have all summer to get ready for school in the fall."

"Have you thought about what you want to do this summer?" Mom asked. I got the impression she had a reason for the question as she asked it.

I thought about that question for a moment. "Not really, Mom. Probably the same things I did last year. Spend time exploring with Krypto. Read a book or two. Work on the treehouse. You know, normal stuff."

"That sounds like fun, Mik. I have another idea, though. Your father and I have been talking and we wondered if you wanted to go to summer camp this year?"

Summer camp? I shrugged at the question. "I don't know, Mom. What happens at summer camp?"

"Well, honey, you go to a camp with other kids. You stay in cabins and get to do all sorts of fun stuff."

"That's right, buddy," Dad said. "You can go swimming and canoeing and learn archery. And you will have camp fires and sing-alongs and stories at night."

That was all sounding pretty good to me. There was something Mom and Dad weren't telling me though. "And you will be there too, right?"

Mom shook her head. "No, sweetheart. It's for kids only. Your dad has to work and I've got to keep the house in order."

I knew it! "But, I don't want to go anywhere without you and Dad," I said. "I need you guys!"

"Mik, you are nine years old," Dad said. "Don't you think

it would be fun to spend time with kids your own age? There will be camp counsellors there to help you whenever you need it. They will teach you all sorts of new things and show you new games and activities."

It all sounded great. But no Mom and Dad? I know I tried to do a lot of things on my own, being a superhero and all, but I always knew they were there for me. I didn't mind admitting the thought scared me.

"But what about Cranberry Flats? What will happen if I go away?" The words flew out of my mouth before I really thought. Of course, Mom and Dad didn't know about my self-appointed role as protector of the town.

Dad looked puzzled. "What about Cranberry Flats, Mik? It will still be here when you come back."

"It's okay to be a little worried, Mik," Mom said. "Dad and I will write to you and you can call us if you get lonely. We're not going anywhere, you know."

"I know, Mom," I said. "It's just that...." I didn't know what else to say without saying too much so I shrugged my shoulders helplessly.

Mom stood and walked around the table and wrapped her arms around me in a hug. "Tell you what, sweetheart. You think about camp, okay?" She pulled out a brochure and gave it to me. "You don't have to make a decision right now. Read through this brochure and we can talk about it again later."

"Okay, Mom," I said, feeling a little relieved. There *was* a lot to think about. Leaving Krypto behind. Who would play with him? And who would look after Cranberry Flats if there was trouble?

"Are you done eating, Mik?" Mom asked.

I looked at my empty plate. I didn't actually remember eating all of my supper but my stomach did feel full. "Yes, Mom."

She collected my dishes. "All right then. Why don't you read up on the camp now while you have time? If you have any questions tonight, we can talk about it."

I got up from the table and picked up the brochure. "Thank you for supper, Mom." Krypto and I ran up the stairs and I flopped down on my bed. I looked at the brightly coloured flyer. On the front it had a picture of a lake surrounded by green spruce trees in the background that came down right to the water. A couple of kids were paddling a big red canoe in the foreground. I couldn't remember seeing such big smiles on anyone before.

I flipped it open and read through it. Camp Sycamore was a summer camp that offered youth the opportunity to commune with nature.

I snorted at that. What exactly did *commune with nature* even mean? It sounded like I would be praying to trees or something.

The next page caught my attention though. It listed some of the activities campers were offered: archery, canoeing, swimming, horseback riding. Those were all things I knew I would love. Indoor cabins, outdoor latrines. The brochure talked on and on about the amenities and lack thereof. No cell phones and no Internet were two items that were clearly mentioned.

Summer camp was sounding better and better, except if I was there, I wouldn't be with Mom and Dad. I also wouldn't be protecting Cranberry Flats. On the other hand, if I stayed home, I couldn't go to camp and do any of the cool things they offered.

I wondered if any of my friends would be going.

It didn't seem to make any difference in what I chose. Either choice had benefits and problems. No matter what I did, I was going to lose something.

And neither choice really addressed the problem of my missing super powers. What were my powers going to be?

Was I going to get one or more powers? When were they going to come?

I tried to ignore the possibility of not having the powers come at all. It was all starting to be too much to think about. I held my head and tried to come up with an answer.

Nothing.

I lay down on my bed and read for a while. I couldn't honestly say what book it was; it might have been a Captain Underpants story, but I'm not sure. Heck, for all I knew, it was just one of my comic books. Whatever it was, my mind kept drifting.

Eventually, Dad came up to say goodnight.

"Hey Buddy. Did you have a chance to read the brochure?"

"I did, Dad. It looks like a really fun place, but I've got to think about it still."

"Do you have any questions before you go to bed, Mik?" Dad asked, coming over to the bed.

"Not right now, Dad. Maybe in the morning though," I said, climbing under my blankets.

"Okay. Well, good night then, Mik. Sleep tight." He gave me a kiss on the forehead and walked to the door. He clicked off the light. "See you in the morning."

"Night, Dad," I said. I snuggled under the covers. When the door shut I realized something. Night vision wasn't my super power.

Ω Ω Ω

I tossed and turned, checking my alarm clock every time I faced it. Time seemed to stand still. I really wanted to knock my clock off the dresser.

Then somehow, I was at camp. I didn't remember how I got there or even deciding to go, but there I was. I was sitting around a fire with a bunch of other kids. Some were singing and others were just sitting next to the fire. It was weird because I couldn't really make out anyone's face.

I was cold and leaned closer to the fire to warm myself. That was fine, except when I started singing with the other kids, the words came out of my mouth and started burning in the air.

I looked around wildly to see if anyone else noticed. As I turned my head, the words flashed out at the other campers and set them on fire. They just sat there, singing and burning!

I tried shutting my mouth and patting the flames out on the other kids, but fire started to shoot out my nose and more things and people burned.

I screamed and a huge burst of flame exploded out of my mouth. Everything was burning. People were dying and I couldn't stop it. I was on fire too, but I couldn't feel it. I dropped to the ground, shouting for help, but no one was coming. I rolled and...

...I woke as I hit the floor. My bedding was wrapped around me like a cocoon. I was covered in sweat and Krypto...well, the poor guy was wrapped around himself in the corner of the room shivering and watching me closely.

I took a deep breath and untangled myself from the covers. I went over to Krypto.

"It's okay, buddy. It was just a bad dream," I said as I held him until he stopped shaking.

I remade my bed and crawled under the covers. "Come on, boy!"

Krypto jumped up on the bed and curled up at the foot. His weight was very comforting and it was late. I felt my eyes growing heavy.

And then suddenly I wasn't in my bed any more. In fact, looking around, I realized I wasn't even in my house.

I was standing in front of the 7-11 wearing my costume. But my costume didn't fit right.

What was going on?

I caught a glimpse of myself in the glass of the store. I stopped and stared.

It was me...but it also wasn't. The balding adult couldn't be me...could he? It was like staring at a mockery of myself. The costume was all too small; my belly was hanging out. I didn't feel super. I just felt tired and old.

And then I heard the laughter and I knew I was ordinary... and a joke.

I woke again and knew it had been a dream. Krypto still slept at my feet. But the dreams, nightmares really, made me wonder which was worse. Having a power that killed people or no power at all.

Okay, that wasn't true. I knew I didn't need powers to be a hero. I would rather be plain old Mik Murdoch for the rest of my life than hurt anyone. I just really wanted powers, was all.

I lay in bed for a few minutes. It was still early and I wondered if I would go back to sleep. I should have known better. In the end, Krypto and I got up and got ready for the day.

I grabbed a quick bite of breakfast before Mom and Dad were out of bed. It was still Dad's day off from the feed-mill and I wanted to let him sleep in. I left a note on the table for Mom telling her Krypto and I were going to do some exploring in the morning and work on the treehouse later in the day. That was usually my weekend routine anyway, but I thought it was a good idea to tell her, just the same.

Krypto and I went for a walk around town. One of the benefits to living right on the outskirts of town was I didn't have far to walk. I didn't do regular patrols like Spider-man or Batman, only because Cranberry Flats is small enough that I could get everywhere over the course of a week and I walked or biked around town all the time.

We took one of our regular routes that goes past the 7-11 store. I thought it might be worthwhile to do a little more superhero research in the comic book aisle when we got there. My plans changed as we got closer to the store, because something didn't quite feel right as Krypto and I got nearer. This wave of...something seemed to reach out to me making me both scared and angry at the same time. When we rounded the corner I saw a bunch of older kids, both boys and girls.

That really surprised me because it was still pretty early in the morning. Most of the teenagers I knew didn't even get out of bed until after noon on weekends. But these kids plainly had something important afoot given the hour. The kids were standing in a circle around two girls. The bigger girl was definitely a teenager. The other looked like she could be my age.

I was still half a block away but I could hear the two girls screaming at each other. The bigger girl grabbed the smaller one by the hair and swung her fist at the girl.

A wave of...something washed over me. It was like I was physically being hit by the anger and malice of the kids. I staggered for a moment before I was able to keep walking forward.

The other kids were cheering and urging the two girls on. The bigger girl punched the smaller one several times. The smaller girl was trying to cover her head with her arms.

I kept walking closer, trying to think of a solution. It didn't matter who started the fight but it was obvious that someone was going to get hurt. My bet would have been on the smaller girl.

I staggered again as a tearing pain shot through my head. My vision dimmed and it was all I could do to keep from falling. The pain was worse than the few times I had been hit with migraines.

The pain disappeared and I could see again, but not the two combatants. The teens surrounding them blocked them from my view. I could hear screams for help and crying coming from somewhere in the circle.

But, what could I do? I was nine years old and there had to be more than a dozen teenage boys and girls in that circle. The 7-11 clerks were watching wide-eyed through the store's windows.

I could try to pull those girls apart, except I'd dealt with girls before and they could be just as mean as boys. I would only get myself and probably Krypto hurt without doing any good whatsoever.

I had to bring adults into this. It made the most sense to run to the police station, especially since it was only a block away.

The pain slammed into my head again, worse than before. I didn't even have a chance to cry out before I fell and darkness consumed me.

Chapter 3

When I woke again, I was lying on the couch in my own house. The whole incident with the fight seemed like some sort of bad dream, except standing around me were my parents, a police officer I didn't know and my friend, Mr. Clancy.

"Mik? Mik are you awake?" my mother asked. She was kneeling beside me putting a cool cloth on my forehead when my eyes opened. I'm not quite sure what it was, maybe it was the way she spoke or looked at me, but I knew she was frightened.

"Mom? What's going on? Why are you all here?" My head felt fuzzy and I was having trouble focusing. "Did I do something wrong?"

"No, Mik. We're all just worried about you," Mr. Clancy said. "First Krypto shows up alone, barking and yapping, at the fire hall where I'm washing one of the pumpers off and then he leads me to a big brawl outside the 7-11 where you happen to be laying on the ground."

"Yes, Mik. Can you explain what you were doing at the fight?" the police officer asked, stepping closer to me.

I shook my head carefully, in case it still hurt. "I can't tell you very much, Sir. Krypto, that's my dog, and I were out for a walk. When we got to the 7-11, we found the fight. I was trying to figure out what to do when I got such a bad pain in my head that I must have fallen down."

"So, you weren't involved in the fight?" the officer asked.

"No, Sir. I was about to go over to the police station. I'm smart enough to know I couldn't have done any good myself."

The officer smiled at that. "I'm glad to hear you know when to get help. It seems your dog knows too." Just like my mom, he seemed afraid. As I thought that, I realized that everyone in the room was afraid. But how could I possibly know that?

"He is pretty smart," I said as I tried to understand what was going on. I reached down to where Krypto lay beside me and scratched at his ears. Krypto leaned into my fingers and sighed. He at least felt normal to me.

"Mik, just so I understand, you weren't involved in the fight at all?" Dad asked.

"No, Dad," I replied. What was going on?

"I think that bothers me more than the thought that you were hurt in a fight," he said.

Mom nodded. "I've already made an appointment to meet Dr. Casey at the hospital." She looked pointedly at the men. "I need to take Mik right away, so if you are done asking him questions?"

The hospital? Why would Mom want to take me to the hospital? I wasn't in the fight. I just fell down. That didn't make any sense at all!

The officer nodded. "I understand, Mrs. Murdoch. I only

have a couple more questions before I let you take Mik to the hospital." He looked right at me. "Mik, did you recognize any of the kids?"

His question made me forget about the hospital for a moment and I shook my head. "No, Sir. They were all teenagers. I didn't recognize any of them."

"If you saw any of them again, would you know it?"

"Oh yes, Sir. I definitely would!"

"Very good, Mik." He nodded at my mother and father. "Thank you for letting me speak to your son. I hope you don't mind if I check in again to see how he is doing?"

"Of course, Officer Steve. Thank you for coming by." My father shook the police officer's hand. "And if Mik remembers anything else, I will be sure to let you know."

"Thank you, Mr. Murdoch. I appreciate that." The officer turned to leave. "I can let myself out."

Mr. Clancy followed the officer. "I'd better get back to the fire hall. I've still got some work to do." He smiled at me and Krypto."You two sure make a great team. You take care Mik. I'll be checking back on you soon."

I waited until the two men had left the house before I asked the question that was nagging at me. "What happened? Why are we going to the hospital?"

"What do you mean?" Dad asked. "Mr. Clancy followed Krypto and found the fight and you on the ground unconscious. We want to take you to the hospital to make sure you're all right."

"Yes, but what happened in the fight?" I asked. "And why wouldn't I be all right? I only fell down. It's no big deal!"

"It sounds like the police came and broke up the fight. I think the kids all ran away," Mom said. "And you falling down when nothing has happened to you IS a big deal. Things like that don't just happen for no reason."

I had a sinking feeling I knew what the reason might be. Was it possible that the magic berry was responsible? Maybe it had gone bad over the weeks I had kept it in the drawer. Maybe the effects were only temporary and I just needed some sleep. I tried to get my parents' minds off the idea of taking me to the hospital. "Is the young girl okay?"

"Young girl?" Mom asked.

"Yes. It was bigger kids picking on a girl who was about my age. A bigger girl was punching her."

"I don't know," Dad said. "Officer Steve didn't say."

"I hope she is okay," I said. "The bigger girl was really hitting her a lot."

"Mik, right now we need to get you to the hospital," Mom said. "Your father will see what he can find out while we are there."

"But I feel fine! I don't need to go to the hospital. Honest, Mom."

Mom looked carefully at me. "Mik, it is my job to make sure you are safe and healthy. Your father's too. Something strange just happened to you that we cannot explain. Something that might be very serious. You are going to the hospital to be checked out. If there is nothing wrong, then I will bring you home. If there is something wrong, then we will do everything we can to make you well." She took the cool cloth and wiped my forehead. "Either way, Mik, you and I are going to the hospital. Is that understood?"

I nodded. It was clear I wasn't going to change her mind. No matter how much I protested. Still, I had to say something. "Will you check on the girl, Dad? See if she is all right?"

"Sure thing, buddy," Dad said. "Now, you listen to your mother and go to the hospital. We need to know why you fell down unconscious."

Ω Ω Ω

The trip to the hospital took less than ten minutes. It freaked me out a little, because Mom kept looking at me like she expected me to explode or something. I was actually glad to get to the hospital; I'd never seen Mom act so oddly or seem so afraid.

When we got there, Dr. Casey was waiting for us at the admitting desk. As much as the hospital scared me, Dr. Casey didn't. He has been my doctor for as long as I have been alive and he has always been nice to me.

"Milly, Mik, how nice to see you," Dr. Casey said, meeting Mom and me as we walked in. He looked closely at me. "What's this I hear about you collapsing, Mik?"

I shook my head and shrugged, trying to get the idea that Dr. Casey was worried out of my mind. "I don't know, Dr. Casey. I was near some kids who were fighting and I got this massive headache. I guess I collapsed because the next thing I remember is I was at home, waking up on the couch."

Dr. Casey looked at my mother. "Do you have anything to add to Mik's story?"

"No, Dr. Casey, I'm afraid I don't. Mr. Clancy, he's one of the volunteer firefighters, found Mik on the ground near the fight. He didn't see Mik at first, but after the kids all scattered, only Mik was left laying on the ground."

"Well, let's get you into an examination room, Mik, and I'll take a look, okay?" He led Mom and me over to the admitting desk. "You two fill in the paperwork while I get us a room. I'll see you in a few minutes."

Mom took the clipboard from the receptionist and filled in my information. By the time she was done, Dr. Casey was ready with a room.

He boosted me up onto a paper-covered examination table. "So, Mik. Let's take a look at your head first." He gently probed my head with his fingers and felt under and along my jaw. He made a humming sound as he examined me.

I relaxed as he worked. I don't know if it was the humming or his gentle touch that did it but I felt better being there.

When he was done with my head, he had me take off my shirt and lay on my stomach. Then he ran his hands up and down my spine, pressing softly as he went.

"I don't feel anything, Mik, and I don't see any bruising, but I don't want to just rely on a physical examination. I think we should also do an MRI.

An MRI! That sounded scary. "What's that? Do I have to?"

Dr. Casey laughed. "Don't worry, Mik. An MRI just lets me look inside your body like an X-ray so I can make sure you are fine. It uses a magnetic field and radio waves to create a detailed image of your body"

"Will it hurt?"

"No, Mik. You won't feel a thing. I promise."

I looked at my mother. "You'll be there with me, won't you?"

Mom smiled her encouragement at me. "I'll be there too, Mik."

"Just not in the same room," Dr. Casey said. The magnetic field is very strong and only the person being scanned is allowed to be in the room."

He led Mom and me into a different part of the hospital. The sign over the door said *Diagnostic Imaging*. A woman, dressed in hospital scrubs, was sitting at a desk filling out paperwork.

She looked up as we entered the room. "You must be Mik," she said. "My name is Shirley and I will be doing your scan today."

I nodded, not quite sure what to say.

Her smile was kind. "There's nothing to be afraid of, Mik. I've done hundreds of these scans and I've never lost a patient." I got the sense that she really cared about me as she was speaking.

That made me feel a little better. "Will it hurt?"

"Not even a little." The expression on her face was serious. "Now, before we are able to do the scan, I need you to change into a hospital gown and take any metal off like necklaces, jewellery or watches, okay?" She grabbed a blue gown and handed it to me. "There's a bathroom just over there to change in," she said, pointing at the bathroom door. "You can just leave your clothes in there.

I nodded again and went into the bathroom to change.

When I came out dressed in my gown, Shirley helped me up onto a table that had a round, donut-shaped machine at one end. "Okay, Mik. Please lie flat on your back and make yourself comfortable. This scan takes a little while, so I need you to be very still."

I lay down on the paper-covered table and shifted my body until I was more comfortable. "And, it won't hurt?"

She smiled. "Nope. Not even a little. You will hear a tapping sound as the machine runs. Don't worry, that's normal. The round part will move up and down your body as it scans you."

"Okay," I said, feeling a little tense.

"Remember, Mik. Lay still. This will take a little while to complete." Shirley checked me over and left the room.

I lay there wondering what to expect. That question was answered when the machine started to make a tapping sound. The big round piece slowly began to move down my body starting at my head. I tried to lie very still.

I didn't feel anything and quickly got bored. I closed my eyes to rest and wait.

When I opened them again, the scan was done and Shirley was shaking me awake. "See, that wasn't so bad was it?"

"No," I said, shaking my head and sitting up. I felt like something was missing but I couldn't be sure what. "What happens now?"

She helped me down from the table. "You go get dressed and join your mother out in the hallway. Dr. Casey will call you when he is ready."

I did as Shirley asked, got dressed and went to sit with my mother. It seemed like forever before Dr. Casey called us back into another examination room.

"Milly, I'm happy to say we can't find anything wrong with Mik," Dr. Casey said. "I'm going to have a nurse come by to do some bloodwork and then you can go. If we find anything we will give you a call. In the meantime, make sure Mik takes it easy and gets lots of rest."

"Thank you, Dr. Casey. I really appreciate your help," Mom said.

"My pleasure," Dr. Casey said, shaking first Mom's hand and then mine. "Take care of yourself, Mik. I don't want to see you again until your next checkup, okay?"

I grinned. "Okay, Dr. Casey. Thank you."

He nodded and left the room. Mom and I waited a few minutes before a nurse came in.

"I understand I need to take a little of your blood," she said. She pulled out a long rubber band and took my arm, wrapping it around my right bicep. "You're going to feel a little poke when I take your blood, okay?"

I nodded. I didn't really like needles, but I didn't freak out from them either.

The poke, when it came, was so small I almost missed it.

I watched with fascination as the vial filled with blood. The nurse pulled the needle from my arm when the vial was full by first covering it with some gauze. She had me hold the gauze while she labelled the vial and then she secured it with some sticky cloth tape.

"Keep the gauze on for an hour or so and no heavy lifting, all right?" She smiled as she spoke.

"All right," I said. I looked at Mom. "I guess the garbages will have to wait until tomorrow."

Mom laughed. "We'll see. Thank you, nurse."

The nurse nodded and collected her things. "You're welcome. I'm sure Dr. Casey will be in touch with you in a couple days with the results."

Chapter 4

I **woke up** the following morning feeling completely normal. For most people that would be a good thing, especially after visiting the hospital the day before. For me, it was a disappointment. Normal meant no super powers.

Just to be completely sure, I checked myself thoroughly in the mirror. My body had a complete lack of anything new. No wings, scales, extra eyes, tentacles, oversized muscles or anything else that might give me spectacular abilities. There wasn't even a bruise where I had my needle.

I tried to hide my disappointment as I went downstairs for breakfast.

"Mik? I wasn't expecting you down so early," Mom said. She was sitting at the kitchen table sipping a coffee when I walked into the room. Her mug was halfway to her lips when she spoke.

"Huh?" I said in my most intelligent way. "Today is Monday, isn't it?"

"Yes it is," Mom said. "But I expected you would want to stay home today after yesterday's excitement."

I shook my head. "No, I feel fine, Mom."

"Are you sure?"

"Yes, Mom. I'm fine. I want to go to school."

"Well, okay," my mom said. "I guess it's all right. But if you start feeling badly, you go to the nurse and get someone to call me. I will come and get you."

"Okay, Mom." I hurried through my breakfast so I could get to school.

Ω Ω Ω

When I got to school I found some of my friends crowded around the bulletin board.

"What's going on, guys?"

My friend, Tony, was the first to speak. "You'll never believe it, Mik. Dr. Hubert Gough is coming to the school this Friday to speak to us for an assembly!"

I thought about that for a moment. The name sounded familiar, but I couldn't immediately place it. "Who?"

Brian, one of my other three friends standing there, looked at me like I had just grown a second head. "What do you mean, who? Dr. Hubert Gough? You know, the scientist who spent all that time searching for the Loch Ness Monster?"

That was enough to trigger my memory. Of course I knew who Dr. Gough was. I lightly smacked my forehead. "I don't know how I could have forgotten!"

"We only spent two months putting the report and display together, Mik," Rahesh, my third friend, said. "How could you have forgotten that?"

He was right. It had only been a few short months prior

that we had done the report. It just showed how rattled I was that I hadn't remembered. "Sorry, guys. I had a lot going on yesterday. I wasn't really thinking."

"Speaking of yesterday, did you hear about the big fight by the 7-11?" Brian asked, leaning in closer to me.

"Yeah, that was part of my excitement," I said. "I was there when it happened."

Tony's eyes got really big. "Really? What happened? Were you in the fight too?"

I was about to speak when a voice behind us spoke up. "Shouldn't you boys be getting on to class?"

The voice was one I knew well. Mr. Long the school Principal. The same man who had once expelled me when another student pushed me into a teacher, breaking that teacher's leg.

He obviously hadn't been paying too much attention to who we were because he stiffened when I turned to face him. His expression went from friendly to stormy.

"Sorry, Mr. Long. We were just talking about the assembly on Friday," I said. I smiled hoping he would finally be over our one-sided feud.

"Murdoch!" I suddenly felt angry, but it wasn't my anger. I don't know how to really describe it. It was almost like when you are watching someone yawn. You don't feel like yawning, but then you do anyway in response to their yawn. All I knew was, I went from excitement at Dr. Gough's visit to where I really wanted to scream at someone.

The feeling was so overwhelming, I could barely spit out two words. "Mr. Long!" I nodded my head to acknowledge I was in fact who he said I was.

"We were just going, Mr. Long," Rahesh said. He must have realized I was angry because he grabbed my arm and pulled me along with him.

The anger only diminished as we got further away from the Principal. It was replaced by fear, surprise, shock and a few other things I couldn't quite identify.

"Are you crazy, Mik?" Rahesh said, stopping to look at me. There was actual fear in his eyes. "You can't take a tone like that with Mr. Long. He'll crucify you!"

"Me?" I said, still feeling angry. "We weren't doing anything wrong. I wasn't doing anything wrong! What is his problem?"

"Dude, he's the Principal. He doesn't need to have a problem," Tony said.

"You better hope he wasn't paying any attention to you," Brian added. "If he was, you will be in trouble for sure."

I took a deep breath and tried to calm down. The problem was, the more I thought about the little incident, the angrier I got. I also felt more confused by a jumble of emotions.

I let the guys lead me the rest of the way to the classroom, forcing myself to keep breathing. I hoped Mr. Long hadn't heard the anger in my voice when I spoke his name.

I was settled in my desk and the bell had just rung when Ms. Millikin, the school Secretary's voice came over the classroom intercomm. "Ms. Killarney, could you send Mik Murdoch down to the office please?"

I sighed. Obviously Mr. Long had heard. I got up from my desk and felt a wave of curiosity and anxiety from all around me. I looked at Rahesh who just shook his head.

Ms. Killarney stepped up to the intercom and pressed the talk button, waving at me to go. "Mik is on his way, Ms. Millikin."

I left the classroom and gently shut the door behind me. This wasn't going to be fun. I briefly wondered if it was too late to go home and call in sick.

I knew it was, but I thought it anyway.

I slowly made my way to the office, dreading every step. I mentally kicked myself for losing my cool in front of Mr. Long.

As I got closer to the office, I realized that I wasn't the one who should be sorry. Mr. Long had been wrong about me before and he couldn't take it. For some reason, he seemed to think it was okay for him to not apologize for his mistakes. It was okay for him to be wrong but it wasn't for anyone to point it out to him.

With every step, I got more and more angry and frustrated with, what I was sure, was going to be a *very* unpleasant discussion with the Principal.

Maybe it was time for someone to stand up to him! He was just being a bully, after all. I felt like a gunfighter about to step out into the street at high noon.

By the time I reached the office, I had worked out what I was going to say to Mr. Long. It was time he got what was coming to him!

I wasn't expecting the look of sympathy and kindness that Ms. Millikin gave me. It washed over me and left me feeling confused. I was still angry, but that anger had left me and was now outside of my body. I had to stop and remember where I was.

"Mik, Mr. Long had me call your mother. You need to sit on the bench until she gets here," she said.

My mother had been called? All because Mr. Long didn't like...well there were so many things Mr. Long didn't like, I wasn't sure where to begin.

So, I sat and waited and watched the clock. I could still feel anger around me, but inside I only felt numb.

It took Mom about twenty minutes to arrive. She looked flustered when she came in and didn't see me seated behind the door on the bench.

"Hello, Ms. Millikin. Can you tell me what's going on?" Mom asked as she came in. "Is Mik all right?"

"Hello, Mrs. Murdoch. I'm sorry, I was only asked to call you in to see Mr. Long. Mik is waiting behind you."

Mom turned and faced me. "What's going on, Mik? Why does your Principal want to see me now? Are you okay?"

I shrugged. "The only thing I can think of is he didn't like the way I said his name before class."

Mom looked confused and started to speak but stopped herself before any sound came out of her mouth. She shook her head. "No, I will hear this from Mr. Long."

While Mom was talking to me, Ms. Millikin was on her phone. She waited until my mother turned to face her again before she spoke. "You and Mik can go into the office now."

I got up off the bench and followed my mother into Mr. Long's office. He came around his desk when we walked through the door and held his hand out to my mother. "Thank you for coming in, Mrs. Murdoch."

Mom shook his hand. "What is this about, Mr. Long?"

Mr. Long indicated a chair for Mom to sit in and went back to his chair. "I called you in because Mik has been very disrespectful lately."

"I see. Can you tell me what he has been doing?"

Mr. Long sighed. "Today was just the latest episode. He and some other boys were loitering in the hallway just before class. I asked them to get to class. Mik ignored me and continued to talk to the other boys."

"What?" I said. That wasn't right.

Mom gave a warning look and I went quiet. "My apologies for my son's outburst, please continue, Mr. Long." The room suddenly felt a lot colder and I shivered involuntarily.

"As I was saying, Mik ignored me. So I told them all to get

to class. That was when he stared at me and disrespectfully said my name."

"Did he go to class?" Mom asked.

"Yes," Mr. Long said. "But that isn't the point. The point is, he was rude to me in front of other students after not listening the first time I spoke to him." Mr. Long seemed to be getting angrier. My head started to ache.

"I see," Mom said. Her calm didn't waiver. "Is it possible that Mik and the other boys didn't hear you the first time?"

"No, they had to have heard me," Mr. Long said. "I was standing right behind them when I spoke." He did not raise his voice, but I got the feeling he was getting frustrated.

"I see," Mom said again. "And how was Mik rude to you?"

"I just told you! He ignored me and then disrespectfully spoke my name." The feeling of anger intensified.

"How did he say your name?" Mom asked. My mother remained calm but I felt like I was in the middle of a storm. Flashes of anger were battering at me from Mr. Long and then I would get gusts of icy calm from Mom.

My headache grew worse as the two adults talked.

"He almost spit out my name before he left!" Mr. Long said. "He did it in front of his friends. I could feel him defying me."

"You...felt him defying you? What exactly does that feel like?" The icy gust struck me again.

"Mrs. Murdoch, I'm not sure you are hearing me. I cannot be any more plain! Mik ignored me and mocked me in front of other students."

"I thought you just said he said your name," Mom said.

Mr. Long's face turned red and a blast of rage slammed into me. I stumbled back, banged into the door and slid to the floor. "Stop arguing!" was all I managed to say.

"Mik! Are you all right?" Mom said, jumping from her seat and coming to kneel beside me.

I could only shake my head. The pain in my brain was too much. I blinked away tears.

"We're going home, right now!" Mom said firmly. She helped me to my feet and led me stumbling out of the office. Mr. Long stood at his desk and watched, his mouth hanging open.

ΩΩΩ

"Mik, what was that all about?" Mom asked as she drove me home.

The pain in my head fled as soon as we were away from Mr. Long. "I don't really know, Mom. Tony, Brian, Rahesh and I were reading the bulletin board and Mr. Long came and told us to get to class."

"And did you ignore him like he said you did?"

I shook my head. "No, Mom, I promise I didn't. I said hello to him and even smiled at him. I thought maybe today might be the day that we could stop being enemies." I looked out the window. "I guess I was wrong."

"What do you mean, you thought today you would stop being enemies?" Mom asked. I felt a small stab of concern and sadness coming from her when she said it.

"I don't know. It just seems Mr. Long doesn't like me very much. It got worse when Lillian was tormenting me last year," I said.

"You mean, it got worse after Mr. Long had to apologize for not listening to you and expelling you from school."

"I suppose." I looked at my mother. "To be honest, I did snap at him. But I didn't do it at first. It only happened after he saw me and started scowling. When he did that, I suddenly felt so mad, I could hardly stand it."

Mom pulled into the driveway of our farm and parked the truck in front of the house. Then she turned to face me. "Mik, it isn't fair Mr. Long treats you differently than he does the other students. He may not even know he is doing it. However, I do think you need to spend the last week or so of school at home."

"But, Mom, Dr. Gough is doing a presentation at the school on Friday! I can't miss that. It's all about his expedition to find the Loch Ness Monster. The guys and I worked so hard on that project!"

"Sorry, Mik, but you are still looking pretty pale and there is no point making you deal with Mr. Long any more than you have to," She climbed out of the truck and I followed her into the house.

"Mom, I've gotta go! I really want to hear what he has to say."

"No, Mik. You gave me a real scare yesterday and today didn't make me feel any better. I need you to stay home until you are feeling better. Maybe next week if you feel all right you can go for the last three days of class."

"But, Mom, that will be too late for Dr. Gough. I will have missed his presentation!"

Mom shrugged. "Maybe your friends can tell you about it."

I knew then I had lost the battle. I felt crushed. "May I go lie down?"

"Of course, sweetheart. I think that would be a very good idea."

I trudged up the stairs and climbed into bed. Krypto jumped up and lay down at my feet. This had to be the worst day ever. I find out one of my idols is coming to school only to have my chance to meet him snatched out of my hands. Now I would never get to meet him.

I could feel Krypto dosing off to sleep. I lay thinking about that. How could I feel my dog falling asleep? I never could before. I focused on him and a wave of drowsiness hit me. It was so strong I closed my eyes and fell asleep.

Chapter 5

"Mik, are you awake?"

I opened my eyes to see the blurry image of my mother peeking around the door. I sat up in my bed. "Hmm? What's up, Mom?"

"Sorry to wake you, honey, but some of your friends are downstairs asking about you. They want to know how you are."

"Tony and Rahesh?" I knew it had to be them. There was something about Mom that told me it was them.

Mom gave me an odd look. "Yes. How did you know?"

I shrugged, still wondering about that myself, wondering what it was about her that gave away the answer. I looked away, swinging my legs over the bed, avoiding that Mom look she gave me. "I think they said they would come by after school."

"You think?"

"I'm still waking up, Mom. I don't quite remember."

"Do you want me to tell them to come back later?"

"No, I'll come down. Just give me a minute, please."

"Okay, Mik. We will be in the kitchen when you come down." Mom closed my door as she left.

I dragged myself out of bed, trying hard not to disturb Krypto. It didn't matter. He was off the bed and waiting at my door, tail wagging, before I stood.

I found the guys in the kitchen just as Mom had said. They were sitting around the table, a glass of milk in front of each and a large plate of cookies in the middle of the table. A third full glass sat at the lone empty seat.

"Hey, Mik," Tony said when he saw me. Cookie crumbs sprayed out of his mouth as he spoke. Gross!

"Hi, Tony. Hi, Rahesh. How did things go at school today?"

"Okay," Rahesh said. He stopped speaking and looked at my mom. I knew he wanted to say more, but not in front of her.

Mom seemed to sense that too because she got up from the table. "You boys stay and talk. I've got some laundry to fold." She left the three of us to stare at each other for a few moments while she left the room.

The rumbling of my stomach got me moving again. I sat down and grabbed a cookie.

"You okay, Mik?" Rahesh asked.

I shrugged. "I guess. As okay as I can be when I'm going to miss the assembly on Friday." I took a drink of milk to hide my face.

"Really?" Tony said. "Why?"

"Did Mr. Long suspend you again?" Rahesh asked.

"No," I said, shaking my head. "At least, I don't think so.

We didn't quite get that far in the conversation before Mom and I left."

"Then, why?" Tony asked again.

"Mom doesn't think I'm well enough to go. I didn't really get a chance to tell you guys much about the fight on Sunday. I don't really even know all the details. All I do know is, I collapsed and Mom took me to the hospital. Now she's all worried and protective of me." I felt a little embarrassed to admit it. "You know how moms are."

"Tough break, Mik," Tony said. "Friday's assembly is going to be awesome!"

Rahesh nodded sadly.

"Tell me something I don't know," I said. I thought about the unfairness of it all. Then I had another idea. "Hey, I know. One of you guys could record it and bring it over so I could watch it."

"Record it with what?" Rahesh asked. "Don't you remember, since that kid Donny broke one of the school video cameras, no student is allowed to use them unless he is a member of the video club? Since none of us are, we aren't allowed."

"Use your cell phone," I suggested.

"That won't work, either," Tony said. "Mine can't do video."

"And my parents won't let me take mine to school," Rahesh added.

I sat back in my chair and sighed. "What a ripoff! I finally get the chance to see Dr. Gough and now I can't because of some stupid fight."

"And because you collapsed and went to the hospital," Rahesh added helpfully.

"Right," I agreed. "I don't know how I could have forgotten that." But I knew the guys were too concerned to hear the sarcasm in my voice. I could feel it in the way they looked at me, and the way they didn't.

"Speaking of forgetting," Rahesh said, "I'd better not forget to give you the homework Ms. Killarney sent for you." Rahesh reached into his backpack and pulled out a small stack of slightly rumpled sheets. "Here you go."

"Homework? You've got to be kidding! There's only a week of school left. We're not supposed to get homework with a week left!"

Rahesh shrugged. "Don't look at me. Ms. Killarney told me to make sure you got this. It's not even stuff we went over today. I checked."

I sighed again. It really felt like someone had it in for me. "Thanks, Rahesh."

Tony grabbed the last cookie. "I'm glad you are okay, Mik, but I've got to get home."

"Me too," Rahesh said. They both stood up and grabbed their backpacks.

"Will you come by again to at least tell me about the assembly," I asked.

"Sure thing, Mik," Tony said.

I walked my friends out the door and watched them ride their bikes out of my yard. It just wasn't fair.

Ω Ω Ω

Friday, the guys came by after school to tell me about the assembly.

"Mik, you will never guess! Dr. Gough is going to be doing another expedition," Tony said. We were in the living room this time, hanging out and watching television.

I turned off Nickelodean and looked at Tony. "Did he say where he was going? Is he going to be posting his daily expedition diaries on the Internet like he did last time?"

"He didn't say where he was going. He said it was a secret to keep reporters and curiousity seekers away," Brian said. "I don't remember him mentioning whether or not he was going to be posting the diaries or not."

"He did and he is," Rahesh said. "He said he would be putting a webpage up sometime next week."

I shook my head. "You guys are so lucky! I wish I could have been there."

"He had pictures of his Loch Ness expedition," Brian said. "He even had underwater video and sound from some of the searches. It was really cool."

I sighed. "Thanks for trying to make me feel better."

"But, I wasn't...." Brian stopped speaking when Rahesh lightly punched him in the arm.

"So, Mik, do you know if you are coming back to school next week?"

I shook my head. "I don't think so. I haven't had any more problems and I feel okay, but Mom and Dad have decided that, since we really don't do anything the last few days of school, I can just stay home."

"That's too bad," Tony said. "Do you know what you're going to be doing this summer?"

"No. Mom and Dad asked if I wanted to go to camp, but ever since last weekend, they haven't mentioned it again. I think that means it won't happen. How about you guys?"

"I've got band camp," Brian said.

"Me too," Rahesh said. "I think we leave next week Friday for six weeks."

"That could be fun," I said. "How about you, Tony?"

Tony grimaced. "We're going on holidays to the Grand Canyon with friends."

"Wow!" I said. "I've never been there. That should be amazing."

"You might think that," Tony said, "but you would be wrong. We're driving all the way there in a van. That will be seven people the whole way in one vehicle."

"But they are friends, right?" I asked.

"Friends of my mom and dad. I'm the only kid going with six grown-ups. It is going to be awful."

I began to understand why Tony wasn't excited. Being the only kid, he would have to keep himself entertained. After a week stuck at home by myself, I could sympathize with him. It wouldn't be easy and he would probably have to be on his best behavior the entire time.

Then it dawned on me. "None of you are going to be in town for the first part of summer vacation?"

"I guess not," Rahesh said. "But you'll be fine Mik. There's plenty to do around here."

"But you guys won't be here to do it with. That won't be any fun."

My friends all looked glum, but only Rahesh spoke up. "Sorry, Mik, but there's nothing any of us can do. I don't have a choice about camp and I doubt that Tony or Brian have a choice either. It won't be for all summer. We'll see you before school."

"You're right, Rahesh," I said. "That doesn't mean I like it." I tried to smile. "At least we can get together until you guys go, right?"

"Yeah," Tony said. "We can hang out tomorrow and Sunday and then every day after school next week."

Chapter 6

My friends and I have often talked about what it would be like to stay home from school. After a few days home, only seeing friends for a short time after school, I can tell you what it's like in a single word — boring. Yes, I had Krypto and my mom home with me, but I couldn't really do much. I even thought it would have been better if I had school work to do, but being so close to the end of the year, there wasn't much of that either, and I'd burned through what Ms. Killarney had sent home pretty fast.

Naturally, Mom wouldn't let Krypto and me go exploring around town. Not when the other kids were still in school. It didn't matter those kids were having game days and an assembly with Dr. Gough.

I really wished I could have been at school to listen to him speak. I was sure he would be talking about his expedition to Scotland to find the Loch Ness monster.

But, I couldn't. Ever since I ate the berry that was

supposed to give me super powers, I'd been crazy with fainting and nearly ready to cry with headaches.

So, I made the best of my time at home, reading and playing games with Mom and Krypto. I helped Mom get the garden ready and I vacuumed the house within an inch of its life.

By the third day, I *had* to get out. At least for a short patrol around town.

When I was sure Mom and Dad were asleep, I put on some warm clothes and slipped out my bedroom window onto the roof of the porch. From there, I climbed down the big tree next to the house and met Krypto on the ground (he used his dog door to get out of the house).

The night was cool and I was glad for the extra clothes. Krypto and I ran to the treehouse to get geared up for our patrol.

I was glad I had cleaned the treehouse a few days earlier. It meant I was able to find everything quickly. I pulled on my costume, which was made up of a loose blue shirt, a red cape, gauntlet gloves and a monster mask. I also put my utility backpack on under the cape. It held my collection of weapons and tools.

Unfortunately, I didn't have much of either in the treehouse; I had cleaned most out for the winter. I had to settle for my listening ear, which let me hear things from a distance, some rope and the dried out cow pies. The power LED on the listening ear glowed a sickly yellow-green colour indicating low power. I might have a few minutes at best to use it.

Not much, but I wasn't really expecting any trouble.

I should have known better.

I left Krypto locked in the treehouse. You might think that was cruel, but I didn't want him waking Mom and Dad up in the house and this was my first patrol in months.

I wasn't sure what he would do. Krypto didn't like it, but he had water, food and a warm bed to curl up in while I was away.

Everything was great for the first half hour of the patrol. I made it all the way downtown. I kept to back alleys and unlit streets to avoid being seen just like I always did. I was just about to the 7-11 when I thought I heard a noise.

I stopped and looked around for a hiding spot. I'm not your typical hero. I'm not big and strong. At least, not yet. Experience had taught me to look first and act second.

I knelt down behind a dumpster and pulled my listening ear from the backpack. I left it turned off to preserve power while I tried to make out what might have made the noise.

For a good minute I didn't hear or see anything. The alley was dark with just the slightest hint of light from the sliver of moon and I couldn't see into darker spots against the buildings.

Then I heard the faintest whisper of air, like the sound a spray can makes.

There was only a single blast of it followed by the sound of furious whispering and a slap. I turned on the listening ear and trained it toward the sound.

"...someone will hear you, dummy! Didn't you hear someone walking down the alley toward us?" The voice was definitely female. I had no idea how old she was.

"I don't hear anything," a male voice grumbled. "Geez, you didn't have to hit me!"

"So, what do we do now?" Another male voice asked. This sounded deeper and much older voice than the first guy.

"I've got to finish this graffiti," the first male said. "If it doesn't get done, we don't get paid and that Punjab in the 7-11 will think he doesn't need protection."

Punjab in the 7-11? Did the unseen guy mean my friend,

Mr. Dhillon? That wasn't right! Mr. Dhillon and his wife were some of the nicest, hard-working people I knew. And protection? What *was* going on here? It certainly sounded like a lot more than just graffiti. It sounded like they were extorting people I knew and cared about."

"Shut up and be still. We wait to see if whoever is out there decides to do anything. If he or she does we'll...." The girl's voice faded out.

I looked down at the listening ear. The LED was dark. The battery was dead. Naturally it would die just as I was getting information. And graffiti? Not in my town!

I pulled out the dried out cow pies and stowed away the listening ear in the backpack. I had to hope the element of surprise would help me out. Except, they seemed to know I was out here. That meant less surprise. They wouldn't be expecting my weapons though.

The cow pies weren't optimal. Squishy, wet and soft was best and these were anything but. Still, squishy wouldn't have worked in my backpack. I would have to make do.

I hefted the first one and thought about how to best throw it. Normally I would have tossed it like you would a regular pie, but these were too light for that. I decided on a frisbee-style throw.

I purposely threw the first one a little high because I didn't know how well it would fly. I needn't have worried though. It flew straight and true. I heard the dull smack as it hit the back wall of the 7-11 store.

"What was that?" The speaker, the first male, didn't even try to be quiet. The first cow pie had the desired effect, obviously scaring him.

I felt a strange bit of lightness pass through my mind. It was weird but over almost before I felt it.

I grabbed the next pie and tossed it directly at the sound of the voices, lower this time.

Another thud as it struck something, but not a wall this time.

"Ow! What the heck was that?" Again it was the first male speaking. I heard the sound of sputtering.

"Whoever you are, you'd better get out of here," the girl's voice called out. "There's six of us and we are gonna mess you up if you don't leave now!"

I was pretty sure that was an exaggeration. I threw another cow pie, aiming toward her voice. Another thud followed by cursing.

A bigger wave of light-headedness struck me. This time it felt more like when it happened the first time at the fight. I swayed a bit but stayed on my feet.

At the sound of their footsteps, I started to run. My weapons weren't working and I couldn't defend myself against three attackers.

"You had better run!" the girl shouted from behind me. "When we catch you, you're going to wish you'd never been born."

I wracked my brain, trying to come up with a plan, but there was nothing. Another flash of *something* spun through my brain and I stumbled. I had to find somewhere to hide. I knew I couldn't outrun them. I could hear their steps getting closer.

Why had I left home without any kind of backup plan? That was a mistake I hadn't made since the first time I went out on patrol more than a year ago. Was there really something wrong with my brain or had I just gotten careless?

A wave of dizziness and fear hit me and I stumbled again. This time I wasn't able to stay on my feet.

I rolled as I hit the ground, and ended up in someone's bushes. I struggled to get back on my feet, but my cape was snagged on branches.

My pursuers got closer.

I only had seconds to get up and away. If I failed, the graffiti gang would catch me and I would be done. I pulled on my cape again.

It stayed snagged.

There was only one thing I could do. I slipped out of the cape and crawled directly into and through the bushes. Branches slashed at my hands and arms as I fought my way through. I felt slaps against my mask and body. I was lucky to have my head covered.

I managed finally to get through the bushes. I jumped to my feet and ran through the neighbour's yard, not stopping until I was almost to my treehouse. I made sure not to take a direct route home, stopping to listen for my pursuers.

I'm not sure when they stopped chasing me. I'm not sure what happened to my cape.

Then it hit me. I had lost my cape! Sure, it had been necessary, but what kind of hero tosses aside his costume and runs away from bad guys? What kind of a hero goes into a fight without a backup plan?

Maybe there was something seriously wrong with me. The doctor said no, but he could be wrong. What if I was finished as a hero? How would I know for sure?

Would I be able to protect Cranberry Flats anymore? Nine years old and washed up as a hero. And not even any super powers.

I trudged the last bit home feeling stupid, foolish, and sorry for myself. I let Krypto out of the treehouse and went to bed. It was late and I was tired but it still took me a long time to fall asleep.

Ω Ω Ω

The following morning, Dad came up to my room and woke me up.

"Okay, Mik. Time to get up and get dressed."

I turned in my bedding to face him, barely awake and wishing he would just go away. "Why? What's going on?"

Dad gave me a knowing smile and flipped my blankets off the bed. "That's for me to know and you to find out. You have to get up, get dressed and get those teeth brushed. Once you are downstairs, then your mother and I will tell you about the surprise."

"A surprise? What is it?" Despite myself, I slid out of bed. The floor was still cold and I hopped back in almost immediately.

Dad grabbed me from my bed and deliberately set me on the floor. He held me there while my feet cooled off. His grin was wicked. "I'm not telling until you come downstairs."

I grinned back. I couldn't help myself. As tired as I was, despite failing my duties as a hero and after days of laying around, something was about to happen. From the way Dad was acting and feeling, I could tell it was something big. Something he was excited about too.

"Okay, Dad, you win," I said. I struggled out of his grasp and raced to the bathroom and locked the door.

He went back downstairs while I rushed through getting dressed and ready for the day. By the time I made it to the kitchen, he was halfway through a cup of coffee. Mom placed a plate of bacon and scrambled eggs in front of me as I sat down at the table.

I ignored the food. "So, what's the surprise?"

"Eat first," Mom said in that tone she has. You know the one. It means: *nothing will happen until you do what I want.*

I ate my breakfast, hardly tasting the food.

When I had finished, I held up the empty plate for my parents to see. "Now will you tell me?"

"Would you like some more?" Mom asked. I could tell she was teasing me.

"*Please*, will you tell me now?" I begged, humouring her.

Dad put his coffee cup down. "Well, since you ask so nicely...." He looked at Mom.

"Honey, we know how hard the past few days have been for you being cooped up in and around the house. We also know you understand why it has been necessary," Mom said.

I nodded, not sure what to say.

"Your mom and I know how much you and Krypto love to spend time outside, exploring and playing in the treehouse. We also know that you need some rest and lots of sunshine."

"Rest?" That didn't sound so good although the sunshine was okay. "What do you mean?" I asked.

"The results came back from your bloodwork," Mom said. "The iron in your blood is low and you don't have enough vitamin D in your system."

Low iron and not enough vitamin D? It was sounding worse and worse. "What does that mean?" I tried not to sound afraid, but I don't know if I did a very good job.

"It means that part of the reason you are feeling tired all the time is because you need more iron and vitamin D. Part of that can be solved by giving you more vitamins and part of that will be helped by you spending time outside," Dad said.

I started breathing normally then. "I don't mind taking vitamins. That will be okay. And Krypto and I can spend more time outdoors."

Dad laughed. "I didn't think we would have trouble convincing you to go out and play. But what would you say if I told you the outside wouldn't be here?"

Somewhere else? Were they sending me to camp after

all? That would mean no Mom and Dad and probably no Krypto. Not a disaster, but hardly what I hoped for.

"Before you ask, no we are not sending you to camp," Mom said.

Not for the first time, I wondered if my mother had the ability to read my mind. "So, what am I going to do?"

"We," Mom put special emphasis on the word, *we*, "are renting a cabin at Lake Osowegol. Since your father still has to work at the feedmill, he will be coming back here during the week and rejoin us on the weekends. We will be out at the cabin all summer."

I looked at Dad, hardly believing my ears. A summer at a cabin at a lake? How awesome was that? *And*, I would still have Mom, Dad and Krypto around.

Dad nodded, a big grin on his face. "We heard your friends are going to be out of town and your mom and I thought it would be fun if we spent the summer at the lake.

"Will there be bears and wolves and cougars and stuff to see?" I asked.

Dad smiled and shook his head. "No, Mik. The lake we are going to has none of those animals. Bobcats and raccoons. Maybe coyotes and deer. That's about it."

I sighed. "Too bad. I would have liked to have seen some of those animals."

It was Mom's turn to shake her head. "Not too bad, Mik. If those animals were around the lake, you would not be going outside alone."

I hadn't thought of that. We don't have any of those animals around Cranberry Flats so it had never even come up.

"Don't you worry, Mik. There will be plenty to do. You can swim and canoe and explore and do all sorts of fun stuff." Dad leaned towards me in a conspiratorial fashion. "And

I've heard there is a lake monster at Lake Osowegol called Naitaka. Maybe you and Krypto could solve the mystery of the creature?"

It all sounded too good to be true. I could only nod my head with what I was sure was a silly grin on my face. Maybe this break was what I needed to get back in the heroing game. I sure hoped so.

Chapter 7

"Are we there yet?" I asked the question as a joke. I've heard that particular question a lot on television.

Dad looked at me through the rear-view mirror. "You're kidding right? We've only been on the road for half an hour."

I grinned. "I'm just joking, Dad. I thought you could use a laugh."

"Stop teasing your father," Mom said. "You know how much he hates being distracted when he drives." I saw the brief wink she gave Dad and sensed the hidden laughter at some inside joke the two shared.

Dad smiled at the wink and I felt him relax. "Don't worry about it, buddy. I'm pretty excited to get out to the lake too. I think we are all going to have some fun."

"Yeah! We can go fishing every day and hiking and canoeing and—"

"Whoa, whoa, whoa, Mik! We can definitely do all of those things this summer, but we won't be able to do them every day. Remember, I still have to go to work."

I wasn't about to let that stop my enthusiasm. "I know, Dad. But even on those days when you have to work, Krypto and I could do a lot of it."

Krypto stirred on the seat beside me and stretched at the mention of his name. His emotions were still fuzzy from sleep. I scratched him behind his ears. "Go back to sleep, boy. We're not quite there yet."

Krypto leaned into my scratching for a few moments before he lay his head back down on his paws and went back to sleep.

"That's true, you can do most of those things while I'm gone," Dad agreed. "But, there are a few rules that you need to follow while you are at the lake this summer."

Rules? Since when did having fun at the lake have rules? "Like what?"

"Well, for starters, you have to always wear a lifejacket when you are out on the lake in any kind of boat," Dad said.

"Lifejackets? Check," I said. It made sense. I'm a good swimmer but I know better than to go into deep water without a lifejacket.

"I would also prefer that you have someone with you when you go canoeing or kayaking or anything on or in the water."

"Does Krypto count?" I asked.

I could feel the unhappiness from Dad before he even answered me. He sighed. "No, I'm afraid Krypto doesn't count as another person, Mik. It has to be another human being. That could be me or your mom or someone else who knows how to handle the boat."

"But...Mom isn't going to want to go canoeing with me all

the time!" I said. I was already starting to see this summer vacation wasn't going to be quite the funfest I thought it would be.

"I'll go out with you sometimes, honey," Mom said.

"You would go fishing with me?"

"Well...maybe not fishing," Mom said. "I would be happy to paddle around and take pictures with you though."

"And you can fish from the shore, you know," Dad said. "That way, you can do both canoeing and fishing. Just not necessarily at the same time. It will be all right."

"Whatever you say," I said, sitting back in my seat. It all sounded pretty boring the way they were describing it. Still, it was better than being cooped up in the house all summer. I pressed my face against the glass of the truck's window and watched the landscape go by.

Ω Ω Ω

The ride out to the lake wasn't too bad; I napped with Krypto for the first bit. Sure, there was country I hadn't seen before, but trees and fields start to look a lot alike after a while.

The car slowing down was what finally woke me up. That and the change of sound from tires on asphalt highway to tires on gravelled road. I looked at the car's clock. We had been on the road for almost two hours!

I sat up, rubbing my eyes.

"Good timing, sleepyhead," Mom said with a smile. "We are almost to the lake. I was going to wake you, but you beat me to it."

I yawned. "I had a feeling we were getting close, Mom." I looked out through the front windshield, but I could only see trees lining a narrow gravel road. "How much longer?"

"Oh, I expect it will only be another few minutes," Dad said, glancing back at me through the rearview mirror.

I'd travelled with my parents long enough to know harassing them for a more accurate answer never worked. There are times when I'm bored that I do it just to add some excitement, but usually I simply sit back and wait for the inevitable to happen. I decided that maybe I should let the summer vacation start on a happy note and I kept quiet.

Trust me, it wasn't easy.

After what felt like hours, we turned off the gravel road onto something that more resembled a dirt path. The truck bucked and bounced along the rutted road in a teeth-rattling way and then, there it was. The lake spread out before us as we crested a final hill.

It was beautiful! Sparkling blue and grey in the sunlight, with patches of beach alternating with trees and waterweeds. I rolled down my window and stuck my head partially out of the car. The sharp tang of spruce trees spiced with the sweet scents of wildflowers and a hint of grass and earth struck my nostrils. I breathed in deeply and sat back in my seat and watched a pair of robins harass a hawk.

I looked back out at the lake. A sailboat was near the far side of the water and a pair of pelicans soared near the middle. As I watched, one folded its wings and dove down into the ruffled surface.

I could hardly wait to jump in and go swimming. Maybe not being in Cranberry Flats would be okay. A twinge of guilt hit me as that thought rolled through my mind. Who would look after the town while I was gone?

I mentally shook myself. I couldn't think like that. Cranberry Flats would be fine.

"How much farther until we get to the cabin, Dad?" I asked.

The words were out of my mouth before I had a chance to think about how wise it might be to ask the question.

"Not much further, if my directions are correct," Dad said. When I paid attention, I could tell he and Mom were both as excited as I was to get there.

Dad manoeuvred the truck down the bumpy road to the lake's edge and followed it for another few minutes before turning in to park beside a two-story, off-white wood-sided cabin. It was about half the size of our house and looked pretty old. A newer shed sat a few strides from the house.

The yard was pretty big, starting at the road and going all the way down to the lake in a gentle slope. Trees bordered it on either side and the grass of the yard was patchy and filled with weeds. The spots without grass and weeds looked like they could be mud pits. A tattered badminton net, hung between two posts fluttered between the house and the lake. A worn path came out of the trees from one side of the yard, followed the beach and disappeared into the trees on the other side of the yard.

My heart sank a little when I saw that. I know, at home, Dad likes to have a perfect lawn. This one was hardly that. I imagined that some of my time would probably be spent mowing and cleaning up the yard. If for no other reason than to keep mud out of the house. Mom's pet peeve.

As soon as the truck stopped, I was unbuckling my seatbelt, opening the door.

"Don't go too far, Mik," Dad said, before my feet had a chance to touch the ground. "Your mom and I will need your help getting all of our stuff into the cabin."

"But—"

"No, *buts*, mister. You have all summer to explore. Right now, we have to get everything into the cabin so your mom and I can start putting things away."

I hung my head. So close! But, I knew better than to argue. "Okay, Dad."

I went around to the back of the truck and waited. Dad came around and opened the truck canopy and endgate. He started handing me suitcases.

"Please take these into the cabin. Your mother will tell you where to put them."

I started to drag the first along the ground.

"Mik! Please carry them. I don't want the bags to get all dirty, okay?"

I lifted the suitcase up and started struggling forward. "You got it, Dad!"

I helped Dad take all of our gear onto the cabin's porch. It was a LOT! There were suitcases, boxes of food, boxes of bedding, dog food, lifejackets and fishing gear. Basically, everything a family would need at a cabin. Mind you, it did have to last us all summer.

When I had delivered the last of the bags (with Dad's help), Krypto and I decided the best place to start our exploring was right in the cabin. "Mom, which room is mine and Krypto's?" I asked.

"There are three bedrooms in the cabin from what your father told me," Mom said. "The biggest is ours. You can pick from the other two, okay?"

That sounded fair. "Okay, Mom." I carried my suitcase upstairs.

It was an easy choice of rooms. I found Mom and Dad's right away. The second room, right across the hall, would never work. It was filled with boxes and bags and practically everything you could think of: a stuffed moose head, old chairs, paintings, chests and a really cool telescope. This was a room I would be investigating more.

Just not right now.

That left the third room. I could only hope it was emptier than the other one.

It was just down the hall from the master bedroom, next to the bathroom. I opened the door and knew I was home.

The room wasn't as big as mine, but it had a nice big bookcase filled with books. There was a neatly made bed under a big pair of windows that looked out onto the lake. A battered old chest of drawers and a small desk and chair completed the furnishings.

Everything I needed.

I put my luggage on top of the dresser and checked out the lake view.

A red, fibreglass canoe rested on a low rack alongside a sun-bleached shed. Beside it lay a white rowboat. The shore was grass right up to the water's edge with a short dock built out into the lake. An aluminum fishing boat bumped gently into it with the movement of the water.

Very promising.

I turned my attention back to the bookshelf. I knew I couldn't spend all of my time outside exploring. What was there to read?

The first book I pulled out was a Hardy Boy novel. That boded well. I love the Hardy Boys. Then I saw a book titled, *Naitaka: Mystery or Monster*. Naitaka was the name of the lake monster Dad mentioned. I pulled it out of the bookcase and opened it up.

The book was one of those really big ones filled with illustrations. I opened a page at random and found a picture depicting several people in a canoe. Towering over them was a creature with a long smooth neck, huge black eyes and teeth that appeared to be longer than any of my fingers. It was snarling and water was dripping off of it.

I read the caption next to the picture: *Artist Rendering of Naitaka attacking early settlers, 1856.*

Wow! It was all so cool! It reminded me of the report Brian, Tony, Rahesh and I had done about Dr. Gough and his expedition to find the Loch Ness monster.

That thought reminded me of the assembly I had been forced to miss. Would I ever get a chance to meet Dr. Gough?

I thumbed through the book some more. There were a few photographs from the 1950's. They were blurry and indistinct, showing...something in the water. From the looks of it, it could have been a lake monster or it could have been a partially submerged log. I simply couldn't tell.

I'm not a cynic or anything. I've seen some pretty amazing things in my career as a superhero, but I try really hard not to believe everything I see. Still, it was pretty incredible stuff.

I promised myself I would read this book from cover to cover and that Krypto and I would investigate and, hopefully solve the mystery of the creature mentioned by both my dad and this book. This was going to be fun!

My thoughts were interrupted by the clap of thunder. Thunder?

I looked out the window. The bright sunshine was gone, replaced by almost complete darkness. I had been so interested in the book, I hadn't even noticed the weather change.

I stood and looked out the window. The once calm lake was now a roiling mass of dark water and white-tipped waves. I knew I hadn't been reading long. I was amazed how quickly the weather changed. I would have to be careful with that.

Chapter 8

There wasn't any point in going outside to explore. Not with the storm blowing. So I took my book and lay down on the bed to read.

It was amazing stuff!

The book began with archaeological reports talking about pictograms showing the monster from hundreds of years ago. There were also cave paintings from the numerous caves that seemed to fill the hills around the lake and one big cliff on the lake had a white stone outline of Naitaka that could only be seen from the water.

If I could convince my parents to let me go exploring, I was going to have a very good summer. I knew about caves though. They weren't to be messed around with. I partially opened my window to let some of the cool air in when I heard the sound of banging cans from outside. The fact that the noise was loud enough to be heard over the pounding rain made it worth investigating.

I put the book down and padded down the stairs with Krypto following on my heels. Mom and Dad were still busy putting stuff away in the kitchen. They had the radio playing and were singing some old song together.

Parents are weird!

I left them alone and went to the front door. I flicked on the porch light and peeked out the window into the darkness. All I could see beyond the covered porch was the glint of light off pounding rain. No eyes or creatures stood outside the door waiting. It seemed safe enough so I slowly opened the front door.

Krypto went running between my legs and out of the cabin. He only partially made it down the porch stairs before the driving rain chased him back.

I felt even safer then. If something had been out there, Krypto would have been barking like crazy. I think he only rushed out because he had been getting bored in the house. I didn't blame him.

I stepped out onto the porch.

Still nothing make any further sounds or attacked me.

I walked the entire length of the porch, which stretched across the front of the cabin and went around the side to the back. I searched the darkness as well as I could from my vantage point, but still did not see or hear anything. I was starting to think I had lost my mind when the sound of rolling and banging cans sounded out of the darkness.

"Mik?" I could hear my mother calling from inside the house. "Mik, where are you?"

"I'm on the porch around the side of the cabin," I yelled back.

"What are you up to out there, Mik?" Mom asked. "I hope you aren't out in the rain!"

"I'm just trying to figure out what is making all of the

noise out here, Mom." I heard footsteps coming from the front of the house. I turned to see my father coming toward me.

"What are you up to out here, buddy?" Dad asked. "I thought you were up in your room."

"I was reading a book when I heard some banging out here," I said. "Krypto and I decided to check it out."

Dad peered out into the darkness. "See anything?"

I shook my head. "Nope. It's just too dark. "

Dad clicked on a flashlight. "Here, try this out."

I smiled. "Thanks, Dad." I shone the flashlight beam out into the rainy night. Other than rain, rain and more rain, I didn't see a thing.

"Maybe whatever was out there has already high-tailed it to drier ground," Dad said.

"Maybe," I agreed. "I guess I'll check it out in the morning."

"Good idea, Mik," Dad said, taking the flashlight back.

Ω Ω Ω

Even with that little bit of excitement, I didn't have any trouble sleeping. The work to bring all of our clothes and supplies into the cabin from the truck as well as the noises of the storm put me right to sleep.

When I woke up, I had the tattered memories of weird dreams that had monsters attacking the cabin from out in the storm with Krypto and me defending my parents with a wand of light. The funny thing was, it was Krypto and I that looked like the monsters.

Like I said, *weird.*

I pulled my slippers on and Krypto and I were about to try creeping down the stairs. Except, I somehow knew Mom was already up in the kitchen making breakfast. It was like I could feel her downstairs.

But that was impossible.

Krypto and I walked down the steps and checked the kitchen. Sure enough, Mom was there. How did I know?

"Good morning, honey," she said when she saw me come through the door. "Sleep well?"

"All right, I guess," I said, trying to figure out just what was going on. "I had some strange dreams, but that's about it."

"That's not too surprising," she said. "Strange new house. Storm howling outside." She looked out the kitchen window at the clear blue sky. "It looks like it's going to be a pretty nice day today, though. Maybe you and Krypto can do some exploring."

"Maybe," I said. "Right now, I'm going to go out on the porch and see what was making all of that racket last night."

"You might as well eat first, Mik," Mom said. "Knowing you, once you get going, you will forget to eat until you're starving."

I grinned. My mom knows me so well. "Thanks, Mom." I sat down and started eating. French toast is one of those breakfasts I really love, but don't usually have time to enjoy. I forced myself to eat until I was almost bursting. Mom was probably right; Krypto and I had a brand-new place to explore that, if Dad were to be believed, had some mysteries to solve. I might not have time to eat.

I got up and put my plate into the sink. Mom already had it full of hot, soapy water. "Mom, is there a washing cloth I can use?"

Mom smiled. "Oh, don't worry about that, Mik. I will do the dishes today. I know how badly you want to get outside."

"Thanks, Mom!" I said, spinning around and running for the door.

"Mik!" I stopped and turned to look at Mom. "Don't you think you should get dressed first? Maybe brush your teeth?"

Mom has a way of *suggesting* things that, when a guy thinks about it, aren't really suggestions. This was one of those times.

"Good idea, Mom," I said. I ran back up the stairs to quickly wash, brush and dress for the day.

I came back downstairs to find Mom waiting for me. "Whenever you get hungry, remember to come back. I've got lots of bread and sandwich meat in the fridge. And don't go too far today, okay?"

"Sure thing, Mom," I said. Krypto and I slipped out into the entryway and I pulled on my hiking boots. The boots were made of thick leather with a rubberized bottom. I had no doubt it would be mucky outside after all the rain.

I wasn't expecting the oozing sea of mud that surrounded the cabin.

I didn't know what to do at first. Yes, I've seen mud before, but never so much. At home our yard is either grass or gravel. Neither of those things get really muddy and the field for the steers was grass too, so other than a couple spots where the cattle like to roll in the dirt, no mud.

This was much different.

The ground was black and almost oily looking with a layer of water on top. How deep the black ooze went was something I could only guess. Krypto and I decided the best thing to do first was walk around on the porch to see what had caused the ruckus the night before.

The first thing I noticed was Krypto's food dish was empty. That was odd because I had filled it just before bed and I knew Krypto had only eaten a tiny bit. What was going on?

I knew as soon as we got around near the back of the cabin what had made the clattering sounds. The cabin's metal garbage cans were strewn around the yard. They had obviously had trash in them too; it was spread all over the place. The combination of the cans being knocked open and around with the wind of the storm had really made a huge mess.

I groaned when I saw it. This wasn't what I hoped I would see when I came outside.

I felt Dad coming outside before I heard his footsteps on the porch. As he came around the corner of the cabin, his fuzzy morning emotions snapped into focus. I had a pretty good idea what he might say next.

"Oh NO! What a mess!"

I walked over to him. "I know, Dad. I was surprised too."

"But what could have done this?" Dad stepped off the porch, the shock of the scene obviously making him forget that he was only wearing pyjamas, a robe and a pair of slippers.

I tried to stop him, but before I could say a word, he had already put his right foot on the ground where his foot sank completely below the surface of the mud.

"Ugg!" Dad lifted his leg and his bare foot came out of the mud with a sucking sound. His slipper was nowhere to be seen. He had to really pull hard to even do that much and, when his foot popped out, Dad lost his balance. He flailed his arms for a moment and then gravity won. Dad sat down in the mud, his housecoat spreading around him like presents around a Christmas tree.

I held my breath, expecting Dad to curse his bad luck. For a moment I thought he might. He looked startled, sitting in the oozing mud, his arms held out at shoulder height as he tried to keep them out of the gunk.

Then there was a sensation of silliness that bubbled up

moments before Dad began to laugh. It started out as a slow, low chuckle that built until he was almost wheezing for breath. Dad lay down in the mud and started to make a mud-angel.

I couldn't help myself. I started to laugh too. He was a real sight! Completely laid out in the mud, moving his arms and legs in scissoring motions, mucky water and dirt spraying up into the air.

I was laughing so hard, I completely missed my mother coming outside.

"Harold! What on Earth are you doing?"

Dad stopped his cavorting for a moment. "Oh, hello, Millie. I'm just relaxing here. You should try it. I hear mud is very good for the complexion." He grinned.

"Well, don't you dare come into the house looking like that, mister! I will not have my clean floors covered in mud!"

Dad sat up. "Don't worry about that, Millie. I'll have Mik hose me off before I come inside.

Mom sniffed and said something under her breath. I didn't hear what it was, but I could feel her amusement.

"Mik, give me a hand out, would you?" Dad asked, holding his hand out.

I looked at his hand. It was dripping with mud and muck. "No way, Dad," I said. "I'm clean and I'd like to stay that way."

"Really?" Dad said. He flicked his finger at me, sending a splatter of mud that struck my shirt right in the middle of my chest. "Opps! Sorry about that." He grinned. "Now that you're dirty too, how about giving me a hand now?"

I shook my head and grabbed his hand, grunting and groaning to pull him out of the mud. It took a little while, but I got him out. We went around the side of the cabin where I got my revenge for the mud splatter when I used the garden hose to wash him off with icy cold water.

Chapter 9

"Okay, Mik. You get your rubber boots on while I go change," Dad said. "Before we do anything else today, we've got to get all that trash picked up."

"You got it, Dad," I said. Honestly, I wasn't thrilled to have to pick up garbage on my first day at the lake, but I had to agree with him. It needed to be picked up.

I put on my tall rubber boots and went out into the front yard. The mud there was just as deep and heavy as around the side of the cabin. It was a real chore walking because I had to basically unstick my feet with every step.

I walked around to the garbage cans, wishing I had been smart enough to make the trek on the porch. That would have been much easier walking. Krypto, of course, had done exactly that, deciding on the easy route after dipping one paw into the mud.

I told you he was smart, didn't I? I wished that I was as smart as him as mud stuck to my boots making them heavier and me taller by the minute. I tried scraping the mud off, but it kept accumulating. It wasn't long before my leg muscles were burning from the effort of walking.

I started picking trash up, and noticed that there seemed to be an awful lot of small animal prints everywhere on the ground. Dad joined me a few minutes later.

"Hey, Mik. Did you see the animal prints?" Dad asked me.

"Yeah, Dad. What do you think they are," I asked.

"I think they are the answer to the spilled trash," Dad replied with a grimace. "Those are raccoon tracks and they are bad news for us."

"Why is that, Dad?"

"Raccoons are very intelligent animals," Dad said. "They can get into almost anything because they have very nimble little paws. They are also very persistent. Once they find food, they stick around until there is nothing left."

"Do they think garbage is food?" I asked.

"Sometimes. They like food scraps like meat and vegetables. Stuff from bags and cans too. I can only guess that's what they found here." Dad stopped speaking to stand up an overturned can. He spent a few minutes scooping up some of the debris that was spread around in the mud.

I thought about that while I picked up trash. "So, what can we do about it, Dad?"

He looked up at me and shrugged. "There isn't much we can do except maybe store the cans in the shed or find a way to lock them so they can't be opened."

That made sense. "Do you think they'll go away if we do that?"

Dad shrugged. "They might, Mik. But, I bet they live close by and will hang around."

"So we have to be careful not to leave anything lying around that they might want to eat?" I asked.

"Exactly, Mik. We will have to feed Krypto inside the house too. They will happily eat his food when he isn't around."

I nodded. "That's probably what happened to Krypto's food. I put some out for him last night and noticed it was all gone this morning." I realized then that I might be the reason for the raccoon raid. "Sorry, Dad."

"For what?"

"I'll bet it's my fault the raccoons are here. I left the food out last night. They probably smelled it and came by."

Dad smiled at me and came over to ruffle my hair. "Don't blame yourself, buddy. I bet those little devils come here all the time. They just happened to get lucky last night."

"Are you sure?" I wanted to believe him, but I still felt responsible.

"I'm sure, son. It was probably more the fault of whoever left the garbage out than Krypto's food."

That made me feel a little better. "Okay, but I'm going to keep Krypto's food and water in the entry from now on, Dad," I said.

"Good idea, Mik. I'll talk to your mom about that when we're finished." Dad straightened up and rubbed the small of his back. "Wow, is this mud ever a pain! I can hardly lift my feet."

"I know what you mean," I said, lifting my foot to show him the mud that stuck to the bottom of the boot.

Dad looked around and scratched his cheek. "I should have expected this when we drove in. No grass usually means mud when it rains unless the ground is gravel. It just stands to reason."

"Maybe it won't rain anymore this summer," I suggested.

"I wouldn't count on that," Dad said. "I have an idea that might fix this though."

"What's that?" I asked.

"I'd rather not say yet," Dad said, trying to be mysterious. "I've got to check out a couple things next week when I'm back in town first."

"Come on, Dad. Tell me."

Dad grinned. "I know how much you love mysteries, Mik. Tell you what. You think about what I might do and, if you guess correctly when I come back next week, I'll bring you a treat, okay?"

"Will you at least give me a hint?"

"Nope. And don't ask your mom, either. I'm going to tell her not to cheat and say anything."

I shrugged. What could it be? I bent down and picked up some more trash. I would think this thing through over the next few days. Maybe I would earn that treat, whatever it might be, by the time Dad got home.

ΩΩΩ

The sun dried out the muddy ground pretty quickly. By the time Dad went to work the next day, there was hardly any wet, clinging dirt left.

That meant, Krypto and I could do some exploring.

Dad put the garbage cans into the shed before he left. We didn't want a repeat of the raccoons knocking garbage everywhere. I especially didn't want to spend my week cleaning up after them while Dad was gone.

I had promised Mom Krypto and I wouldn't go too far the first few days. She was getting used to the new place just like I was. So, when the ground was dry enough, Krypto and I went for a walk along the lake.

In front of the cabin there was a well-worn path that went along the lakeshore. That was where we started.

We hadn't gone very far to the south of the cabin before we found a narrow, but fast moving river with a wooden bridge built to allow crossing. The bridge was tall and would easily allow a canoe to go under without the paddlers having to duck. The pathway continued across the bridge and onto the opposite shore of the river.

I walked to the middle of the bridge and stared over the side into the moving water. I couldn't see anything on the bottom, which made me think it could be pretty deep. I could see where the river fed into the lake. When I looked back, I could only see to the first turn of the water. Thick trees obscured its source. A flash of movement caught my eye, but was gone almost as fast as it appeared. It might have been a girl, but I couldn't be sure.

I looked back down at the water and a dark shape glided under the bridge. I ran to the other side to see if it came out.

Nothing. I rubbed my eyes wondering if I had just seen what I thought I had seen. I waited a few more minutes, running from side-to-side on the bridge, but whatever it was, I didn't see it again.

I knew this was somewhere I would have to investigate. Just not today. I wasn't really dressed for it for one thing and I had promised Mom I wouldn't go too far.

Krypto and I crossed the bridge and walked a bit further down the pathway. We walked for the better part of twenty minutes before we came to another cabin. It looked a lot like ours.

I stood on the path and stared at the cabin for several minutes wondering if anyone actually lived there. I couldn't see or hear anyone around. In fact, I had this empty feeling inside that insisted that no people were there.

I shrugged. Either no one was home or the cabin was

empty. Either way, I was starting to get hungry. I could tell Krypto was too. He kept giving me looks suggesting we turn around. It didn't hurt that I heard his stomach rumbled too.

We went home to spend the rest of the day with Mom at the cabin. When we got back she was just starting to dig a garden patch. I don't know if I've ever mentioned this, but Mom *loves* being out in the garden. Maybe even more than Krypto and I love to explore.

"How come you're digging a garden, Mom? I didn't think this cabin was ours."

Mom stood and wiped the back of her hand across her forehead leaving a dark smudge of dirt on her skin. "It isn't our cabin, sweetheart, but the man who owns it said we could have it for the summer if we put some improvements in. That means painting what needs painting and fixing what needs fixing. He provides us with the materials and we do the work. Understand?"

"I guess so, Mom. But what does that have to do with putting a garden in?"

"Well, Mik, this patch of dirt was just weeds. If I put a garden in, I pull the weeds and we might get some vegetables by the end of the summer. Even if we don't, the ground will be improved from my work."

That made sense to me and I could tell Mom was having fun. Like I said, she *loves* gardening so there wasn't any reason she shouldn't have a good time doing what she liked.

We helped her do some digging for a while until it was lunchtime and then we all went into the house.

I was eating a grilled cheese sandwich when someone honked a big truck air horn. I started to get up from the table but Mom stopped me.

"You finish eating your lunch, Mik. I'll go see what's going on outside."

"But, I want to see what's happening!"

Mom wouldn't hear any of it. "No, Mik. You will have plenty of time to see when you are done lunch. Now, you sit back down and I will go see what's going on."

Her tone didn't leave any room for argument so I reluctantly sat back down and ate my sandwich. I won't deny that I ate more quickly. I guess I thought the sooner I finished the sooner I could see what was going on.

I wasn't fast enough though. Mom was back in the house in just a few minutes.

"What was outside, Mom?" I asked.

"You'll see," she said with a smile. "Remember how your Dad told you he had a mystery for you to solve?"

I nodded and started to grin. "Is the mystery outside?"

"Not exactly," Mom said. "The first part of it is."

"Can I go see now?" I begged. I held up my empty plate. "I'm finished eating?"

"Would you like me to fix another sandwich, Mik?" Mom asked. I could tell she was teasing me. It didn't matter, though. I wasn't hungry anymore.

"No, thank you, Mom." I took my plate and glass to the sink. "Can I go outside now?"

Mom laughed. "Oh, very well. You go ahead, otherwise you are liable to explode."

"Thanks, Mom," I said, giving her a kiss on the cheek. I ran to the entryway and put on my runners. I just shoved my feet into the shoes without bothering to tie up the laces. I couldn't spare the time. Whatever was outside was waiting for me.

Chapter 10

I ran out of the cabin and around the side where I had heard the truck horn. What I saw made me stop and stare, my mouth hanging open.

"Holy cow!" Where the big mud pit had been was an enormous pile of black dirt.

"What do you think?" Mom asked, coming up behind me on the porch.

"It's really cool," I said, imagining the possibilities for fun. "But why is it here?"

"Ah, but that's part of the mystery," Mom said. "You have to figure it out why your father had that big load of dirt delivered here."

I scrunched up my nose as I tried to solve the puzzle. "Is it for your garden?"

Mom laughed. "I may use some of it, but I could never use it all."

"So, what is it for?" I asked. "Come on, Mom. Don't tease! What are we using all of the dirt for?"

"Uh uh!" Mom said, shaking her head. "I promised your father I wouldn't tell. You have to figure out for yourself."

"Can I at least play on it now?"

"Hmm." Mom tapped the bottom of her lip with her right index finger. "You go and change into some grubby clothes and you can play on the dirt. In fact, if you want, you can play on it all week until your father comes home. After that, we'll see, okay?"

"You got it, Mom." I ran into the house to do as she said. What could Dad be planning? The dirt to play in was really cool; it was another thing Krypto and I could do together. But that didn't solve the mystery. I ran the possibilities through my mind. Maybe a big garden for Mom? But she was already planting a garden so that probably wasn't it.

I was going to have to give it some serious thought.

Ω Ω Ω

I had a *lot* of fun on that pile of dirt. I built roads for my trucks, slid down it on my behind and even tried riding my bike up and over it. The downside to the dirt-pile showed up after the first day.

Krypto and I were just stepping up on the porch when Mom stopped me.

"Mik. You hold it right there!"

I stopped. Mom's voice had an, *or else* tone to it. "What's the matter, Mom?"

"You are filthy. Both of you."

I looked down at my clothes. They were dirty; I couldn't argue that. Krypto didn't look quite so bad. He was a little dusty, but that was it. "Krypto's not so bad. I could brush him off."

Mom looked closely at Krypto. "I suppose that would be all right, but as soon as you are done, you are to go straight upstairs and have a bath."

"Okay, Mom," I said. That was the first of a series of baths. Krypto and I didn't get any exploring done, but we did have a great time.

I gave the problem a lot of thought over the following days. My original idea of dirt for a garden was completely wrong; Mom had all of her seeds and potatoes planted by the following day. So what could be the reason?

I thought maybe Dad wanted to level out the ground. That made some sense, but only added to the mystery. If that were the reason for the dirt, why was he levelling the ground? I didn't think it was for bricks or blocks or anything like that. I had helped Dad lay sidewalk blocks a year earlier and he taught me then that sand and gravel were the materials to use for that sort of thing.

So, what was it?

By the time it was Friday, the dirt mound was much shorter and wider. All of our playing had spread quite a bit of it around the yard. I still hadn't figured out what Dad was planning to do with it either.

That was okay. It was fun trying to figure out the mystery while I played.

I had my answer when Dad came to the cabin from work early that evening. He had a flat-deck trailer hitched to the back of the truck and on the trailer were dozens of rolls of grass.

"Hey, Dad!" I said as he climbed out of the truck. "How was your week?"

Dad grinned. "Not as good as yours, I think." He looked at me carefully. "Is there any part of you that isn't dirty?"

"Probably not," I said, laughing. "I think I figured out your mystery."

"Before or after I drove in the yard?" Dad asked.

"Well...honestly, it was after," I confessed. "Is all the dirt for spreading around the yard? Are we putting down grass?"

"You got it, buddy," Dad said. "I thought it might be a lot nicer for everybody if we didn't have a repeat of that mud pit. And we can all enjoy the grass when it has had a chance to root."

He looked over at the dirt mound. "You've done a great job starting to spread the dirt out for me, too."

"I didn't really do it on purpose. It kind of just happened."

"That's okay, buddy. I actually expected it. I hope you had fun on the dirt."

"I did," I said. "I've taken the baths to prove it."

"And, I bet your mom has done the laundry to prove it too."

"I suppose."

"Any more evidence of our four-legged bandits?" Dad asked.

"Four-legged bandits...oh, you mean the raccoons?"

"You got it. Have they been around since you put the garbage cans in the shed?"

I thought about that for a moment. "I've seen tracks around the yard, but that's it. Nothing has been spread around or broken."

"That's good. I'm glad we've got them under control."

"It's mostly good, Dad," I said. "The shed has gotten pretty stinky since we moved the cans in there. Mom wasn't very happy when she first went in there to store her gardening tools."

"I'll talk to her, Mik. Thanks for letting me know." Dad

stretched. "I think I'll go inside and say hello to your mom and wash up for supper."

"What about all of the grass on the trailer?" I asked.

Dad laughed. "I appreciate your enthusiasm, but it's going to have to wait until we have had a chance to spread and level this dirt. Are you up for helping me in the morning?"

"You bet!" It was going to be great helping Dad again.

"All right, then. You should probably get changed and washed up for supper too. Maybe leave some of the dirt from your clothes out here, okay?"

"Sure thing." I followed him to the porch and cleaned as much of the dirt as I could off my clothes and out of my shoes. I could smell the roast Mom was cooking to celebrate Dad's return. It was going to be really nice eating together as a family for the first time in days.

Ω Ω Ω

We all got up early the next morning and began to move dirt around. I filled up the wheelbarrow Dad brought from the farm and he pushed it to low spots on the yard where he dumped it. Both Mom and Dad spread it around while I filled the wheelbarrow with the next load.

Talk about a lot of work! I was ready for a nap less than an hour after we started.

But we all kept at it, sweat running down our faces leaving long, dirty streaks. I knew Dad could be relaxing on his only weekend home with Mom and me and yet we still worked. That meant spreading and levelling the dirt was important to him. That made it important to me too.

We were taking one of our breaks when Dad put down his glass of ice water and looked at me. "Mik, I'm going to need your help with something when I'm gone."

"You got it," I said.

"Hold on a moment, there pardner!" Dad said with a grin. "Don't you want to know what I need before you agree to it?"

I shrugged. "I trust you."

That struck my dad as funny for some reason. Maybe I should have worried. He has been known to play the occasional trick on me.

"Well, Mik. What I need you to do is make sure the grass is watered well every day and that no one walks on it. The water will help the roots to grow for starters. People not walking on it will keep the ground nice and flat. If people were to walk on the grass when it's wet, it will put holes and dents in the ground and grass."

I thought about that for a moment. It made sense. "You can count on me."

"I knew I could," Dad said. He went to tousle my hair and looked at his grubby hands. He changed his mind then and held out his right hand. I shook it solemnly.

I liked it when Dad had jobs for me to do. It made me feel important. Especially when the feelings behind the jobs matched the way he treated them, like now. I could tell Dad was proud of my willingness to help him out.

"Okay then. I guess I'm rested enough to keep working if you are," he said, grabbing his shovel.

Mom sighed and stood, brushing off her clothes. "I'm ready. How about you, Mik?"

I grinned. "Ready whenever you are."

"Then let's get at it. This yard isn't going to do itself."

We worked until almost dark, shovelling dirt, moving it with the wheelbarrow and generally trying to make everything as level as we could. I don't mind telling you, I was pretty tired when we finished. I hardly had the energy to wash up to help make dinner.

ΩΩΩ

I think I remember eating dinner. I think. I don't remember going to bed. All I know is, one moment I was eating and then the sun was shining through my bedroom window. I groggily opened my eyes and looked at my clock to find it was already eight and light.

Great! On the day I was going to help my Dad put in the lawn, I slept in.

I scrambled out of bed and rushed downstairs, sure my parents would both be up and outside working. They looked up at me as I came careening through the doorway into the kitchen. Dad was drinking coffee and reading the newspaper while Mom was working on a crossword puzzle.

"Good morning, buddy," Dad said, lifting his cup in a sort of welcome.

"You're not outside working!" I blurted out before I had a chance to think. Sometimes I am the master of the obvious.

"True enough," Dad said, taking a sip of his coffee. "I will also point out that your mother is not outside working too, just in case you hadn't noticed." He winked at me when he said it.

"That's great," I said. "I mean, I'm glad you didn't start without me."

"Start what?" Dad asked.

"You know. Putting down the grass."

"Oh, that!" Dad said, setting his cup down on the table. "I'm already done. I knew you would want to go out and play or explore today so your mom and I went ahead and did it while you were asleep."

"But...." I didn't know quite what to say. "But, I wanted to help you!"

"Oh, Harold. Stop teasing Mik," Mom said. She gave my father a stern look before she looked at me. "Mik, your father knows you want to help. The grass is still all sitting on the trailer waiting for you two mighty men to do your thing."

"Is that true, Dad?" I demanded, feeling a little betrayed. After all the hard work we had already done together, he thought he would prank me?

"Guilty as charged, Mik," Dad said, looking a tiny bit sheepish. "Sorry, buddy. I couldn't resist." He got up from the table and grabbed me in a rough bear hug. "You've got to understand, I've been away all week. I've got to get my digs in while I can."

I hugged him back. "Okay, Dad. You're forgiven." I disentangled myself from him and waggled my finger at him. "Just remember, you need me to water that grass when you're gone! Don't mess with the help."

He held his hands up in surrender. "All right! I give. Don't be mad. I'll behave."

I had to laugh. It was good having Dad home.

Chapter 11

I ate a quick breakfast and got dressed. Then Dad and I went outside.

I didn't realize laying sod would be such a lot of work. First of all, the grass was heavy! I could lift a roll of grass off the trailer and carry it to its place on the ground, but it was a struggle. And it got more difficult with each roll. It wasn't long before I was sweating harder than when Dad and I were moving the dirt.

I kept reminding myself hard work would make me stronger. That's pretty important for a superhero.

Thinking about being a superhero made me wonder about Cranberry Flats. I hoped the town was all right. I suppose Dad would have said *something* if things were bad. At least I hoped he would.

I also learned something about laying grass I never expected. I thought it would be as simple as unrolling the sod, then putting another right after it. We would keep going until we ran out of yard or grass.

That was true to a point. What I hadn't expected was for Dad to put a handful of fertilizer under each section. When I asked him about that, he explained the fertilizer would help the roots grow faster and stronger, which made sense.

Then he showed me how to curl the ends of the sod down so the two adjoining pieces would come together properly without a visible seam. He also staggered the joins so two rows didn't have their ends at the same place. He did all of this to keep the grass from looking like a patchwork.

It was fascinating!

Krypto lay in the shade of the porch, watching and snoozing. I could tell he was relaxed having his normal dog-dreams. Mom brought us cold drinks and sandwiches at noon and we stopped for lunch on the porch.

Dad was looking out over the grass. I could feel his contentment.

"The grass is sure looking good, Dad."

"It really is, isn't it, Mik. Amazing what a difference a little grass makes."

"Sure does." I took a bite of my sandwich, loving the taste of corned beef, lettuce and mustard, and chewed for a few moments before swallowing. I could tell Dad enjoyed his as much as me. "So, Dad, what do you need me to do when you go back to town next week?"

"I'm glad to hear you ask that question, Mik. It means you care about how this turns out." Dad turned toward me a little where he was sitting. "Well, the first couple weeks are pretty critical for grass. It needs to be kept wet so the roots grow down into the soil. People," he turned toward Krypto, "and dogs need to stay off the grass too."

"Because they might put holes in the grass and soil," I said, nodding my head.

"That's right. It's also a good idea to keep dogs out because sometimes they like to dig. That would make a huge mess."

"No problem. Krypto and I will find somewhere else to play. Oh, and I'll water the grass every day."

"Thank you," Dad said, stretching. "This grass was pretty expensive, so I want it to come in properly."

Expensive? That brought a thought to mind. "Dad, why would you spend money on somebody else's property if all we are doing is staying here for the summer."

Dad actually looked startled at that question. "Well, I made a deal with the cabin's owner, Mr. Massing. He's one of my best customers at work. We get to stay here very cheaply for the summer in exchange for some work around the property. I spoke to him about the grass when I went to town last week and he agreed that could be part of our payment."

That made a lot of sense. "Then I'll be sure to take really good care of it while you're home working so you don't have to replace any of it."

"Thanks," Dad stood up, signalling the end of lunch. "We're almost done. What do you say we get this little job finished and take the rest of the day off?"

That sounded good to me and I said so. I picked up our dishes and took them into the house for Mom. Dad and I got to work then and managed to get all the sod laid before dark. We finished up by rolling the entire thing with a heavy drum to pack and level it all.

When we were finished, Dad gave me a special treat. He led me down to the cabin's dock. "I thought since you worked so hard today, you might like a short cruise on the lake in the cabin's fishing boat."

"Really?" I asked. "That sounds great!" Honestly, I hadn't even thought about the fishing boat since we got here.

Mom was already at the dock when we arrived. She smiled and handed each of us a lifejacket.

"I hope you don't mind going in a fishing boat, Mik," Dad said. "The motor is just a little electric trolling motor, but it will take us where we need to go." He helped Mom into the boat.

"Are you kidding? This will be fun."

Dad lugged the heavy battery into the boat and connected the leads from the motor to it. He showed me how red had to go to the positive pole on the battery and black to the negative (both were marked on the battery, in case you were wondering). We all settled in and Dad guided the boat away from the dock.

It didn't go fast, but we were absolutely noiseless on the water. The loons, swimming near us, weren't even startled by the boat.

It was awesome.

Ω Ω Ω

Dad came into my room when I went to bed that night. "Hey, buddy," he said sitting beside me. "Are you all ready for bed?"

"Yep," I said. Something told me he was unhappy about something. "I had a bath and brushed my teeth." I bared my teeth at him to show the truth of my story and then I smiled.

"Good man," Dad said, tousling my hair. "Listen, Mik, I'm heading back to town tonight so I don't have to get up so early for work in the morning. That means you won't see me until next Friday."

My smile dipped...a lot. Now I knew what was bothering him. I almost protested until I realized just how hard his leaving was hitting him. I couldn't let my Dad leave feeling like he let me down. I threw my arms around him in a big hug.

"Dad, thank you for working so hard for Mom and me," I said. I could feel tears threatening, but I savagely forced them back. Dad was feeling bad enough. "I know that being away from us is hard on you and I know you are doing it so Mom and me have a great summer. I really appreciate it."

I could feel Dad's surprise. He held me away from him and stared into my eyes for a few moments before he finally spoke. "When did you...?" He had to stop speaking and cleared his throat. "Mik, when did you get so grown up?" He held me hard then.

I felt something warm drop on my shoulder and realized it was a tear. Dad's tears. He never cries and I suddenly felt badly what I had just said, was the reason.

"Sorry," I mumbled into his shirt, inhaling the scent of him: soap and the outdoors and something else that was all him. "I didn't mean to make you cry."

He held me a little harder then. I wasn't exactly struggling for breath, but it was a close call. "Never apologize for being perceptive. You are exactly right. I've been struggling about leaving you and your mom alone. You just reminded me how right that decision is."

I felt pretty awkward. I mean, how weird is it to have the kid helping the adult? I just know it felt strange to me, so I changed the subject.

"You don't have to worry about the grass, Dad. I'll take good care of it."

Dad stood and wiped his eyes with the back of his hand. "I know you will, son." He clapped his hand on my shoulder. "Can I tuck you into bed before I go?"

"You bet!" I hopped under the covers, bouncing a little. "I'll miss you, Dad, but I will take care of Mom and Krypto while you're gone. I promise."

"Thanks, Mik," Dad said, tucking the covers snuggly around me. He kissed me on the forehead. "Don't forget to take care of yourself too, okay? Remember, you need to rest so you feel better. I love you."

"I love you too, Dad," I said.

He turned and left the room, clicking off the light and gently closing the door behind him. His mood was much different as he left. Almost...confident. He wasn't exactly happy, but I could feel contentment in him. Maybe because he knew his decision was the right one.

I thought about that. It had felt really odd to talk to my dad that way, but now it felt like I had done the right thing. Would I always know what the right thing to say was? I almost blew it by acting immature and complaining about him leaving.

That's when I had another thought. I knew how my dad had felt. It wasn't that I was perceptive, as Dad had said; I had actually known how he was feeling. I considered the past few days when I had a sense of what Mom or Krypto's emotions had been.

It was the same.

I almost smacked myself in the head with my hand. I did have a super power after all! It had been there all along. It might even have been responsible for my fainting at the fight. My super power — I was almost afraid to admit it to myself in case it wasn't true — my super power was the ability to sense other's emotions.

It had shown me the way in the nick of time.

I would have to pay close attention to what it was telling me in the future to avoid making mistakes when I dealt with people. That thought made me feel both better, and at the same time, more under pressure to think before I acted and spoke.

I guess that's why some heroes feel like super abilities are both a credit and a curse.

Krypto jumped up on the foot of my bed and curled up. His emotions were fuzzy with sleep. I yawned, barely able to keep my own eyes open.

Ω Ω Ω

I woke the next morning chasing the wispy remnants of some very odd dreams. Small creatures ran around in those dreams. They had evil little faces and seemed to get in the way at every turn. Above all, I remembered feeling how very curious they were.

I sat up in my bed, dislodging Krypto from his place at my feet. I thought about my dad and how he had to sleep all alone in our house back in town. I scratched Krypto behind the ears just the way he likes, realizing how lucky I was to have my pal here with me.

"What do you think, Krypto? Should we go water the grass like Dad taught us?"

Krypto cocked his head at me. I'm not quite sure what he thought about going outside with me this early. His emotions didn't really tell me much either.

I swung my legs over the side of the bed and put on my slippers. I staggered out of my room to the bathroom where I did my morning routine. Then I dressed and went downstairs, Krypto following on my heels.

"Morning, honey," Mom said as I came into the kitchen.

I should have known. Mom *always* seemed to be able to get up before me. It didn't seem to matter what time I was up, Mom was there.

"Hi, Mom. Krypto and I are going to go outside and water the grass before breakfast, okay? Dad said we should do it early in the morning or late at night. I thought morning might be best."

"No problem, Mik. I will hold off making breakfast until you two come back in, okay?"

"That's great." I walked into the entryway and pulled my rubber boots on. I didn't want to get my runners wet, after all.

Krypto and I went outside and.... "Mom!" I yelled as loudly as I could. I just stood staring in shock.

I both heard and felt Mom come running toward me. "Mik! What's the matter? What's wrong?" I could feel her alarm.

I have to admit, I was too. I just stared at the yard. Every single piece of sod my dad and I had laid the previous day was now sitting rolled up as if it had never happened.

Chapter 12

"Mik, what's...." Mom's voice trailed off as she saw the grass. I could sense her shock. It closely mirrored my own feelings. She walked slowly toward me. "What in heaven's name happened?"

I shook my head. "I wish I knew, Mom." I stepped off the porch. Every single piece of sod was rolled up and lay haphazardly around the yard. The dirt was still packed down with bits of fertilizer embedded in the soil. I knelt down to take a closer look.

In the dirt were small holes. They were all over in no particular pattern. Little trails ran from the holes. It was very curious. All over the ground were the ever-present raccoon footprints. Here and there were spots where it looked like the raccoons might have dug into the soil.

It didn't make any sense at all.

"Mik, I'm so sorry," Mom said.

"It's okay, Mom," I replied. In truth, it wasn't particularly okay, but what else could I say? I pushed on the closest roll of sod. It dutifully rolled out and lay nice and flat on the ground.

I stood and looked at it for a second. I had honestly thought it would roll up again like a piece of paper but it hadn't. It lay on the ground now like it had never been moved.

I pushed the roll beside it. It too rolled out on the ground and lay flat and still. The grass was almost perfectly laid out next to the first piece I had unrolled.

I nudged that grass so the two pieces fit snuggly together and unrolled a third. Just like the first two, it unrolled on the ground right beside the others.

Maybe it wasn't as bad as I thought.

"Mom, I'm going to try and put all of the sod back down and then I'm going to water it. I think I can get it down pretty quickly. It still seems to be lined up properly and everything."

"Okay, Mik. I'll go get my gardening clothes on and give you a hand." She turned around and walked back into the house.

I looked at Krypto who seemed puzzled by the whole thing. "Hey, buddy. Let's see if we can't get this done before Mom comes out."

I smoothed the dirt and unrolled more grass, moving it a tiny bit whenever necessary to get it tight against the adjoining grass. It was actually going pretty well.

Krypto even tried his hand...I mean, paw...I mean, nose, once. He managed to push the roll out with his nose, but got dirt all over it in the process. That seemed to be enough for him and he retreated back to the porch.

By the time Mom came back out, I had managed to do almost a quarter of the yard.

"Wow, Mik! You have been moving fast," Mom said when

she saw my progress. She pulled on her gardening gloves. "Where would you like me to start?"

"How about on the other side of the grass from me," I suggested. The first roll had been about the middle of the yard and I was working toward one side. "I think it will work better to just keep doing the pieces right next to what is already laid out. That will make it easier to snug the grass together."

"You're the expert, Mik," Mom said with a smile. She got to work where I suggested and was rolling out the grass quickly. I showed her a couple of the tricks Dad had taught me so she could keep the seams invisible.

Between the two of us, we managed to get all of the grass back in place by lunchtime with only a couple breaks in between. I could tell Mom was tired. Honestly, so was I, but I had promised my dad I would look after the new lawn. I put the sprinkler onto the grass to water it while Mom and I had lunch.

After the water was turned on, I sat on the porch and just watched the water go back and forth.

It wasn't long before Mom called me. "Mik! Mik, lunch is ready."

"Thanks, Mom," I called back. I got up and went into the house. "Mom, may I eat my lunch on the porch?"

Mom looked puzzled. "Sure, Mik. Any reason why?"

"Well, honestly I want to keep an eye on the grass," I said.

Mom smiled at that. "I know you promised your father that you would take care of the new grass and I'm glad to see you taking the responsibility so seriously. But what are you going to do at bed time?"

I shrugged. "I don't know, Mom. But the grass being all rolled up doesn't make any sense. Do you think someone is playing a prank on us?"

"Maybe," she said. "We don't know anyone around here though."

"I wondered about that," I said. "So, you don't mind if I eat on the porch?"

"No, sweetheart, I don't. In fact, if you're okay with it, I think I will join you. It is a beautiful day, after all."

"I'd love that, Mom. We could treat it like a picnic!"

"That's a fine idea. Why don't you go and pull a couple chairs from the front around the side and that little table that's with them. I'll bring out the soup and sandwiches."

"Okay!" I ran outside and, with a little grunting, I pulled the heavy wooden deck chairs and table around the side of the house on the porch where we would have a nice clear view of the grass. When I finished that, I moved the sprinkler to get some of the grass it hadn't reached before.

Mom brought out our lunch and we both sat, relaxing and enjoying the food. Krypto, the big mooch, made sure he was nice and close in case either of us wanted to share with him. He wasn't disappointed.

"What are you going to do with the rest of the day, Mik?" Mom asked as we ate.

"I thought I would sit here and read one of the books I found in my room," I said.

"You're not going to go exploring or play? Mik, the weather is beautiful today." I could hear the concern in her voice.

"Mom, honestly, I'd rather sit for the rest of the day. Laying all of that sod twice in two days has tired me out."

Mom laughed at that. "Mik Murdoch! I never thought I would see the day when you were tired. I may have to mark it down in my diary."

"Very funny. Those rolls of grass are really heavy!" I flexed my arm, half expecting the muscle to be twice as large after the two days worth of workouts. It didn't look any different to my dismay.

"They certainly are heavy, Mik. Your father would be very proud of how hard you worked to fix things up. I know he wasn't expecting anything like this to happen."

I felt a little better hearing her say that. In the back of my mind I had been wondering if maybe Dad had rerolled the grass as a sort of prank on me. I should have known he would never do that.

We finished lunch and Mom took the dishes inside. I ran up to my room and got the copy of *Naitaka: Mystery or Monster?* Now was as good a time as any to do some research on the resident mystery. Mind you, I already had a mystery to solve, closer to home. Namely, who, or what, had rolled up the grass?

Chapter 13

Once again, I slept fitfully with lots of dreams. Just like the night before, an overwhelming sense of curiosity filled the dreams of small, evil-faced creatures. I wasn't sure what to make of it all, but I had a dreadful feeling the meaning wasn't good.

I got up and got ready for the day. Then Krypto and I went downstairs. Mom was waiting for me. I couldn't read the expression on her face, but her emotions were pretty clear.

"It happened again, didn't it?" I asked.

Mom nodded. "I don't know who is doing this, but I wish they would stop. Have some breakfast and we can go outside to lay it down again."

I sighed. "Okay, Mom." I really didn't want to do the work a *third* time, but what could I do? I made my dad a promise.

We ate breakfast in silence. I know I was thinking hard about who could possibly be pulling this nasty prank.

Maybe one of the kids from the fight was out at the lake and knew I was here too. Maybe they were doing this to get even with me.

I knew I wasn't going to mention that to my mom. She would only worry more.

And she was worrying. I didn't need a super power to know that.

We went outside, a lot slower than the day before, and got to work. My muscles were aching from the previous two days so I wasn't moving nearly as fast. Neither was Mom.

We took more breaks this time, stopping every thirty minutes or so to have a drink and rest our sore, tired muscles.

You know how I thought the exercise might be good for my superhero career? Yeah, I was really over that plan by the third day, let me tell you.

We had lunch, this time in the kitchen; I don't think either of us wanted to spend any more time looking at grass than we had to. Then, we were back to work.

There was about a third of the grass left to lay when I heard a boat on the lake. It wasn't the first boat I'd heard, but it sounded close. In fact, it sounded like it was getting closer by the minute.

Mom and I stopped what we were doing and went to stand on the porch to get a better look at the lake. Sure enough, a boat carrying two men approached the dock in front of our cabin.

The boat pulled up beside our dock and a young, bearded man in thigh-length swimshorts and a short-sleeved Hawaian shirt jumped out. He grabbed the front line of the boat and tied it to the dock.

I was trying to see who he was but I couldn't quite make him out. He was still too far away for my newly discovered super power to detect how he was feeling, so no help there.

Mom started to walk toward the dock and I went with her. Who could possibly be visiting us?

The man waved and smiled. "Hello! You wouldn't happen to be Mildred and Mik Murdoch, would you?"

Mom smiled at the man. "Yes we are. how may I help you, Mr...?" She left her sentence hanging, waiting for him to fill in the rest.

"Gough, Ma'am. Actually Dr. Gough."

I let out a small gasp which ended up sounding more like I was choking than anything else. Mom turned to me quickly.

"Mik, what's wrong?" she asked.

I had stopped walking. I had to swallow a couple times before I could manage to make my mouth work. "Did you... did you say your name was Dr. Gough? Dr. Hubert Gough?"

I could feel Dr. Gough's amusement before he answered me. "Ah, so you have heard of me."

"Sir, I watched all of your video logs and read everything you wrote about your expedition to find the Loch Ness monster."

Mom, who had stood back to watch me gush, spoke then. "So, you are Dr. Gough." She held out her hand. "It's very nice to meet you. Mik speaks of you often."

"It is very nice to meet you, Mrs. Murdoch," Dr. Gough said, shaking her hand. "You are probably wondering why I'm here."

"The question had crossed my mind."

That seemed odd to me. Not the words, but how Mom felt when she said it. She really wasn't curious at all.

"Well, you see, I was speaking at Mik's school last week. After my presentation, a number of students came to speak to me." Dr. Gough turned his attention to me. "Some of those students were friends of yours. Brian, Tony and..." he had an expression of thinking hard, "and Rahesh, I believe."

I felt a surge of excitement flash through me as Dr. Gough mentioned my three friends. "Yes, that's them! What did they say?"

"They told me how you had really wanted to be at the assembly to meet me but couldn't. They showed me the fine work you all did in your report about me. All of that convinced me that I should stop by your house to say hello."

"That's very kind of you, Dr. Gough, but it still doesn't explain why you are here," Mom said.

The way she said that and the rising sense of laughter that was coming from her convinced me something was up. "Wow!" was the only thing that came out of my mouth.

The doctor nodded. "Imagine my surprise, when I stopped by your house to learn from your father you had already left town to spend the summer at Lake Osowegol. The very lake at which I am conducting my current expedition."

"That is amazing," Mom said.

This time I could hear the laughter in her voice.

I turned to face her. "You knew Dr. Gough was here!"

She shook her head. "Not at first. But late last night your father phoned. He told me about Dr. Gough and how he might be dropping by this week. I wanted the visit to be a surprise."

"Boy, it sure is. I can't believe you are here, Dr. Gough. This is so cool! Are you here to try and find Naitaka?"

Dr. Gough looked and felt surprised. "You know about Naitaka?"

"Mik's father was telling him stories on the way out," Mom said.

"Not just that! There's a great book about Naitaka up in my room," I said. "I could run up and get it to show you?"

Dr. Gough laughed. "Tell you what, Mik. Why don't you and your family come over to my camp this weekend? I can show you around and you can show me your book?"

"Can we, Mom?" I could hear the pleading in my voice, but I didn't care.

"I think we probably can," Mom said, grinning at me. "Mind you, I don't know where Dr. Gough's camp is."

"Don't worry about that, Mrs. Murdoch. One of my assistants will come by Saturday morning to pick you all up, if you like."

"Oh, that would be lovely," Mom said. "Thank you!"

"My pleasure." Dr. Gough held out his hand to me. "I've got lots to do, Mik, so I should be going. I'm looking forward to seeing you on the weekend."

I shook his hand. "Me too, sir. And thank you!"

I watched Dr. Gough leave in his boat and then started to turn toward the grass. Down the path I saw someone running away, back through the trees. The clothes were different, but I was pretty sure it was the girl I had seen a couple days before. I could sense extreme loneliness from the retreating figure. I shrugged. Trying to find her would have to wait. I had work to do.

Ω Ω Ω

It was mid-afternoon when we finished laying the grass but I didn't care. The surprise of seeing Dr. Gough made the time fly by. After all, I was going to tour his expedition site! That was something I never expected to do.

Neither of us were moving as fast by the time we were done but we were working a lot more efficiently. I used the bare minimum of movement necessary to roll out the grass and nudge it into position.

If I wasn't so tired of laying grass, I probably could have gone to work for a landscaping business to put lawns into homes. I would have been good with all of the practise I'd been getting.

When we finished we both went into the house to clean up and go to bed.

I know that sounds strange; we hadn't eaten supper and it was still early, but we had moved several thousand kilograms of grass three times in as many days. Most of my muscles hurt and, judging by Mom's emotions and the way she moved, she hurt too.

Besides. I had a plan.

I had brought my alarm clock from home that I used to wake up for night-time patrols. My clock has a great feature which allows me to plug in a small external speaker , which I did now and tucked under my pillow, something I had done many times at home without my parents being any the wiser.

I had decided to get up after dark to try and catch the grass-rolling villains in the act, and hopefully prevent having to re-lay the sod a fourth time. I wasn't sure my body would survive it.

I had borrowed the telescope from the extra bedroom and set it up in my room. It was my intention to use the telescope to spy on the yard without alerting whoever was doing the dastardly deed. I put on the porch light so I would see what was going on. All I could do was hope there would be enough light.

I set the alarm to go off at midnight and climbed into bed. Would the light on the porch scare away whoever was coming around? I sure hoped not.

Ω Ω Ω

The alarm woke me at midnight just as planned.

So far, so good.

Krypto looked at me like I was insane when I dislodged him while I was getting out of bed. When he started to whimper, I shushed him. I didn't want anything to either wake up Mom or warn whoever might be outside.

I wrapped myself in my blankets and went over to the telescope. I could see some light glowing on the grass that was just at the edge of my vision.

That the grass was still there was encouraging. I was in time to catch the culprits, assuming, of course, that they would come again.

I sighted in the telescope on a brightly lit patch of grass. It was actually pretty cool. I could make out the individual blades of grass.

When I looked away from the telescope and up into the sky, I was sorely tempted to point the device up instead of down. The sky was completely clear and filled with stars. More stars, in fact, than I usually could see at home.

But, I resisted and sat down in a nearby chair to stake out the yard.

I was obviously more tired than I thought.

The weird dreams pulled me out of my drowsing. In fact, I thought I was still dreaming after I woke because the emotions were still so strong. Curiosity and hunger (anyone who doesn't think hunger is an emotion has never been really hungry) assaulted my mind.

I rubbed my eyes and got to my telescope. I was barely in time to see a creature roll the grass up in front of me.

I couldn't believe it! The creature was a raccoon. Probably one of the same ones that had knocked our garbage cans over several days before.

But why? Were they some alien creatures or super-intelligent animals out to make my life miserable? Maybe they were under the control of one of my enemies.

I didn't have to wait long to find out.

Within moments of the raccoon rolling the grass out of my line of vision, it was back. I saw it daintily pick up a nice juicy worm and gobble it down. It ate two more before it moved on.

So that was their game! Somehow those intelligent little monsters had learned that worms came up under the newly laid grass at night. They had learned the lesson and now knew to come around and feast on the wormy bounty.

As much as I admired the little devils, I didn't want to have to keep unrolling and replanting the grass. Something had to be done.

I put my slippers on and ran down the stairs. Krypto came skittering behind me and together, we left the house, whooping and hollering. The raccoons looked up at us, and almost as a single being, turned and ran for it. I think it was the noise and surprise that drove them off.

I didn't expect it would work a second time.

Mom's bedroom light went on and I could hear her calling for me.

"I'm down on the porch, Mom. I figured out who has been rolling up the grass."

I surveyed the damage to the yard while I waited for Mom to join me. I had managed to keep the raccoons from completely rolling all the grass up again. In fact, only about a third of the yard would need to be laid back properly. As much as I didn't like having to do the work again, it was better than doing the whole thing.

Mom came around the porch, her arms and housecoat wrapped tightly around her to ward off the night's chill. "What's going on, Mik?"

I pointed to the yard. "I know what's been doing this now."

She brightened a little at that before she frowned. "Mik! You shouldn't be coming out here by yourself. What if the people who did this hurt you?"

"That's the thing, Mom. It wasn't people at all. It was raccoons. I heard something and came down to see. The raccoons were rolling up the grass and eating the worms underneath."

"Raccoons? What?" Mom looked startled at that.

I grinned. "I wouldn't have believed it if I hadn't seen it."

"So what do we do now?" Mom asked. "I don't really want to be staying outside all night guarding some grass."

I searched for the emotions that had come from the raccoons earlier. Either I couldn't control my super power well enough to locate them or they had run too far away for me to detect.

"I think they are scared away. At least for now," I said. "Besides, I don't want to stay outside all night either."

"Well, one thing I know for certain: we are not re-laying the sod tonight. Come on. Let's get back to bed. We can deal with this mess in the morning."

We both went back to bed and my final thoughts before falling asleep were, *how am I going to keep them from rolling the grass up again?*

Chapter 14

Re-laying the grass the third time was much easier and faster than the previous two days. That was partially because Mom and I were much better at the job than the first few times and also because the raccoons had only managed to roll up about a third of the lawn. We started working on it right after breakfast.

"Mik, you know I love working outside in the yard and garden, but I swear, I hope to never have to do this again," Mom said, wiping an arm across her sweaty forehead. She left a dirty smudge behind.

"I'm with you," I said. "Krypto and I would love to be out exploring and having fun instead of doing this every day."

Krypto raised his head at the mention of his name. He had been napping pretty much every day I worked, figuring out pretty quickly grass wasn't really meant for dogs. His emotions were drowsy...and bored. I knew my buddy wanted to be out as badly as I did. Still, I had something to look forward to now; visiting Dr. Gough's camp.

"Any ideas how we can keep the little rascals away from here?" Mom asked.

I guess since I spent a lot of my time out-of-doors, she thought I might know something about raccoons. I wished I did. I had a feeling I would be learning a lot about the little critters over the summer.

"Not really," I admitted.

"I wonder if turning lights on would keep them away?" Mom asked, more to herself than anything.

I shook my head. "I doubt it, Mom. They didn't seem overly bothered by the light last night."

Mom looked surprised. "Was that on before you came down? I thought I had turned it off before I went to bed."

"I actually turned it back on," I said. "I hoped it would either keep whatever had been playing pranks on us away or let us see who was doing it. It did work for the latter."

"I should have thought of that. Good going, Mik."

"Thanks. Now, if you don't mind, I'm going to have a look around to see if there is anything we can use to keep the raccoons away. Maybe something we can build a fence with."

"Okay, honey. I'm going to go into the house and wash up. I'll make us some iced tea for when you come back in."

"That sounds great."

While Mom went into the house, I checked out the shed. I hadn't really spent any time even investigating the house and yard since I had arrived. This whole sod thing had kept me pretty busy.

The shed held a lot of the normal things you would expect: old hand tools, rakes and shovels, a manual push-mower and the like. Nothing that could really help. In the far back corner of the shed an old canvas tarp covered something. It also had the stink of hot garbage since we were storing the cans in the building to keep the raccoons out. Too bad that wouldn't work for the grass.

I opened the door as wide as it could go to let in the maximum amount of light and let out some of the smell. What could possibly be under there? My imagination surged. Maybe there was some sort of automated raccoon attack robot!

I flipped the canvas off the mystery object and my heart sank a little. There was nothing as spectacular as the imagined robot. In fact, the pile was just a bunch of old camping supplies and a bucket of rusty nails.

Too bad!

I left the shed to have some iced tea. Maybe I would find something good in the basement. I wasn't going to hold my breath though. My luck hadn't been that good so far.

I sat down at the table and leaned on my arms, feeling dejected.

"No luck, honey?" Mom asked.

"Nope," was all I said.

Mom plunked down a glass of iced tea in front of me. "I will call your father and ask him for ideas. Too bad he won't be able to help us until Friday."

"Mom, what could Dad do that we can't?" For some reason, I felt a little offended that I wasn't able to solve the problem and had to look to Dad to save us from our problem.

"Well, for one thing, he could bring some traps or some fencing material or something. Maybe the grass people have something to actually fasten the grass to the ground. I don't know."

Fasten the grass to the ground? That actually sounded promising. But what could we use? I thought about what I had seen in the shed. Nothing really useful there. The camping gear might have some old tent pegs but not enough to do the job.

Then I had it.

The nails!

I could use the bucket of old rusty nails to peg down the grass.

"Mom, don't call Dad just yet. I think I have an idea."

"What are you going to do?" Mom asked, her curiosity plain.

"Let me try my idea out first. If it works I'll show you." I drank down my iced tea in one gulp.

She laughed. "Okay, Mik. Good luck."

Ω Ω Ω

I brought out the heavy pail of old nails and a hammer I had found in the shed. The nails were every size and degree of rust imaginable. Some were even mostly straight. I could only ask myself, *what kind of a warped mind keeps nails like this?*

I picked out a handful of the largest, straightest nails and sat down on the grass, glad I hadn't yet watered it. I pushed the first nail into the grass near a corner and tapped on the nail. It sank down halfway immediately. I tapped a few more times until the nail head was just sticking out of the grass. I put two more nails into the grass on the narrow side, one in the other corner and one about the middle.

I experimentally tried to roll the grass. It moved a little but held firm.

This just might work. I looked at all the grass. This could take a while. I put nails around the edges of the first piece of grass and moved on to the second.

I was working on the third piece of sod when I heard a voice behind me.

"Why are you nailing your grass to the ground?"

I turned to see a girl, about my age, standing, watching me with a puzzled expression on her face. She looked familiar for some reason although I had never met her. Of that I was certain.

"We have a raccoon problem," I said. "We just laid this grass a few days ago, but every night the raccoons come and roll it up again searching for worms."

The girl stared at me for several moments. I probed, just a little, to see what she was feeling. Her emotions were in turmoil, sometimes angry, sometimes curious and a whole lot of other things. I think, and I'm not completely sure here, but I think she was wondering if I was lying to her or not.

I slowly stood. "I'm telling you the truth. Ask my mother if you don't believe me. I'm nailing down the grass to try and stop them. If I can't figure out how to make them leave the grass alone, it will probably die." Probably was almost a certainty. There were already spots where the lawn was turning brown despite my watering it."

"Oh, I see," she said. Her feelings were still pretty wild. One emotion kept rising to the top though: loneliness.

That triggered a memory. I knew where I had seen the girl before. She was the person I had seen twice– once by the bridge when I saw the shadow under the water and then after Dr. Gough left in his boat.

I have to admit, even though I have Krypto here to play with and Mom to keep me company, *and* the grass to keep me busy, I missed other kids. From the emotions I sensed from this girl, she felt the same way.

"My name is Mik Murdoch," I said, holding out my hand like I had seen Dad do many times.

The girl looked at my outstretched hand like it was a snake or something and just stood there, not saying a word.

I wasn't about to be shut down. "My family and I are here for the summer. Are you from around Lake Osowegol?"

The girl shook her head solemnly. Her emotions spiked from lonely to sad. "No. My family and I were staying the summer in a small town by the name of Cranberry Flats."

"Cranberry Flats?" I almost shouted it. She had been in my town!

"Yes. Do you know it?"

"Know it? That's where I'm from," I said. "What did you think of it?"

"It was okay, I guess," she said. "Mom and Dad thought I would have more fun at the lake for the summer, though."

"And you don't think you will?" I asked.

She shook her head. "There isn't anything to do here. Mom won't let me swim or go on the lake by myself and there isn't anyone to play with."

I nodded. "I know exactly what you mean. My parents are the same way with me."

"Oh," she said. She stood and was quiet for several moments. "Would you play with me?"

I didn't really have to think about that question for long. Like I said before, I missed having other kids to play with. "I would love to."

The girl smiled then and I felt her relief. It was like the release of floodgates. She held out her hand. "I am very glad to meet you, Mik Murdoch. My name is Cynthia. Cynthia Deets."

I took her hand and shook it gently. I had learned some girls didn't like me trying to shake their arms off and I wanted to keep my good impression alive. "I'm very pleased to meet you, Cynthia."

"Mik!" I heard my mom's voice seconds before she came

around the corner of the cabin. "Mik, are you...oh, hello!" That last was said when Mom caught sight of Cynthia.

"Mom, this is Cynthia. She is staying at the lake just like us," I said.

"Hello, Cynthia," Mom said, stepping down off the deck. "It is very nice to meet you."

Cynthia looked at the ground. "Nice to meet you too, ma'am."

"Please call me Milly, Cynthia" Mom said.

Cynthia looked horrified at the idea. Her feelings echoed her expression. "Oh, I *couldn't* do *that!*"

"Would Mrs. Murdoch be better?" Mom asked.

"Yes, Mrs. Murdoch, it would," Cynthia said, looking relieved. "My mother would never let me call an adult by their first name!"

Mom smiled. "Would you care to come in for some refreshments? I was just about to ask Mik if he wanted something. You are more than welcome to join us."

"Thank you, Mrs. Murdoch, but I have to get home. I was just out on a walk when I found you and Mik."

Mom's eyebrows rose. "Oh! Are you staying nearby, Cynthia?"

Cynthia pointed toward the path that Krypto and I had walked to the bridge. "I'm just down that way. My mother and I are staying there for the summer while Father works."

"That must be very lonely for you and your mother," Mom said. "Please tell your mother that I would welcome her company for lunch tomorrow if she is able to come."

Cynthia looked excited at that. "I will, Mrs. Murdoch!" She turned and started to run to the pathway. She stopped suddenly and turned. "Thank you! Good-bye." Cynthia waved and ran off out of sight.

Mom watched the girl run off before she turned her attention back to me. "How are you doing out here?"

"Pretty good, Mom. I think I might have a solution that will keep the raccoons from rolling up the grass again."

Mom walked closer to the grass I had been working on. "Are those *nails*, Mik?"

"Yep. There were a bunch of rusty old nails in the shed." I knelt down beside the piece of sod I had just been working on. "Look, I'm making sure that they are sticking out of the grass far enough for us to see so we remember to pull them all out."

"Do you really think that will work?" Mom asked. I could tell she was having a hard time believing my nails would do any good.

I shrugged. "I know they are making it harder for me to lift the grass. I thought I would put a lot around the edges and fewer inside the grass. That should stop the raccoons."

Mom nodded. "How much longer do you need to finish?"

I looked at the grass. "Probably another hour."

"Okay, sweetie," Mom said with a smile. "How about I have lunch ready for when you are done?"

"That sounds great. I want to finish this before I eat anything." I bent down and got back to work hammering nails into the grass.

Chapter 15

I didn't get a chance to find out if my plan worked until the following morning. The last thing I remember is asking myself if I should set the alarm. I must have fallen asleep right after that.

When I saw the sun shining through my window, my first thought was, *Oh shoot! I forgot to get up!*

I hopped into my clothes and ran down to see what damage the raccoons might have done. Krypto was almost running me down in his eagerness to be outside.

I ran around the cabin to check on the grass, afraid that I would see the whole lawn rolled up once again.

Only three pieces of grass were rolled up and those were in the middle where I hadn't put as many nails.

Success!

I did a little dance and Krypto jumped and barked around

me. I hadn't realized just how much the raccoons had been ticking me off.

I ran to the shed and grabbed the hammer and a handful of nails. I made short work of the rolled grass, nailing it even more securely to the ground than it had been.

Those raccoons were certainly smart little creatures. As I was working on the grass, I realized these were the only pieces of sod that I had really skimped on nails with. And those little devils had found them! That meant persistence.

I could respect that, even if it annoyed me. I would have to remember that going forward in my dealings with them.

I put the water on the grass and went into the house in search of breakfast. Mom was, as I expected, already busy in the kitchen. The wonderful aroma of bacon and eggs greeted me when I came in.

"Morning, Mik," Mom said when I came in. "How do things look outside?"

I tried to look sad. "Well, the raccoons were back. They rolled grass up, again."

"Oh, honey, I'm so sorry," she said, bringing over a plate of bacon and eggs. I could feel her dismay washing over me. "I know how hard you worked on trying to stop them. I was sure your plan would work. No matter! You eat your breakfast and we can lay the grass again. Maybe if we put something on top overnight...."

I couldn't let my mom worry about the grass any more. "That's okay, Mom. I've already fixed the problem."

She gave me a funny look. "But, you just said the raccoons rolled the grass up again. How could you have fixed it so fast?"

I grinned. "I said, they rolled grass up, not all of it. They only managed three pieces last night. I've already nailed those back down and added extra nails."

"Only three?" I could feel her delight at that. "That's wonderful!" Mom leaned over and gave me a kiss on the forehead. "You were just teasing me, weren't you?"

"I was," I admitted. "I hope you're not mad?" I knew she wasn't, but I couldn't let her know that.

"Of course I'm not angry, Mik," Mom said. "I'm very proud of you for figuring out a solution to those animal's antics."

"I just hope we've seen the last of them," I said. "I never realized what a mess raccoons could make. They sure are a lot of trouble."

"They certainly are. Almost as much as little boys."

I don't think I was supposed to hear that last bit, but Mom was happy when she said it so it didn't make me feel bad. I supposed that must have been a bit of a mom joke.

She sat down at the table with me and drank a coffee while I ate breakfast. I don't know what it is about bacon, but even when I'm not hungry, I smell some and I've got to eat it.

"So, what are your plans this morning, Mik, now that you don't have to lay sod again?"

I thought about that for a minute before I answered. "I didn't really have anything specific planned. Krypto and I might spend some time down by the lake. We haven't really had a chance to do that much outside."

"You're right. We've all been so busy trying to get settled and keep the grass from running away that we haven't had much chance to do anything else."

"Did you have anything you needed help with before we go outside?"

"Not really. Just remember I invited your friend Cynthia and her mother to come for lunch. I'd like you to be back before noon so you can get cleaned up."

"Mom, I just met her. She's not my friend." As I said it, I

realized it wouldn't be so bad to have someone else to play with. Even if she was a girl.

Mom held her hands up in a warding gesture. "Sorry! I meant, the girl you met yesterday."

"That's better," I said, trying to look offended. I don't think I did a very good job though because Mom just took my empty plate and shoo'd me out the door.

"You and Krypto have fun. I know you're a good swimmer, but, until I know more about this lake, I want you to stay out of the water. Is that understood?" Mom's voice had that firm, no-nonsense tone that meant I had better listen.

"Yes, Mom. I will stay out of the lake." I looked down at my pal, Krypto. "I can't promise Krypto will stay out of the water, though."

Mom laughed at that. "I wouldn't believe you if you did. I know Krypto likes water." She waggled a finger at me. "If he does go in, you will have to come back earlier to give him a bath. I've finally got the cabin clean and I don't want muddy dog in it."

"You got it." Krypto and I headed for the door. "See you before lunch."

"Have fun."

ΩΩΩ

I gave Krypto a quick bath in an old tin tub outside the cabin. Our playing outside had resulted in Krypto getting more than a little muddy as he chased sticks and ran into and back out of the lake.

Mom had thoughtfully left a ragged grey towel and some soap for me to use on my pal. Somehow she just knew Krypto was going to need a bath. That must be another mom power.

By the time I was done, my clothing was dry and I had a strong odour of dog from Krypto's baths: the two shake-offs from by the lake and the one in the tub. We went into the cabin and I quickly got cleaned up and changed.

Now what? Cynthia and her mother weren't expected yet, so what could Krypto and I do while we waited.

I had to quickly correct myself. Do something where we wouldn't get dirty. Having to wash up twice (and bath Krypto twice) was not something I really wanted to do. But what options did we have?

I heard a small snore and realized Krypto had already found his own activity. He looked so contented curled up in a patch of sunshine I almost lay down beside him.

But no! I wasn't the least bit tired and a nap would only make me groggy.

I spied the book *Naitaka: Mystery or Monster?* I hadn't looked at it since I paged through the book the first day we arrived. Things had gotten really busy, what with the Raccoon Menace causing chaos and mayhem around the cabin.

I thought about that for a moment. Raccoon Menace? Was that what my superheroing had become? Trying to defeat a posse of rowdy raccoons?

That thought made me a little sad. After all, back home I defeated monsters, real and created, helped families and generally kept Cranberry Flats safe. It felt a little silly to be battling raccoons after all of that.

I shook myself then. Saving the grass was important. Being a hero meant big and little deeds. Helping my family was just as important as helping my community.

I felt a little better after that. I grabbed the book and lay down on my bed to do some reading on the mysterious Naitaka. After all, if Dr. Gough was here to find the creature, I might be able to help him out if I knew more.

Ω Ω Ω

"Mik, Cynthia and her mother are here!" Mom's voice interrupted my reading and I quickly looked at my clock to see how long it had been. Almost an hour! Hard to believe.

But, the information in the book had been fascinating. Naitaka, if it were real, sounded like a mystery I needed to solve. A serpentine water creature that looked like the dinosaurs of old had apparently lived in the waters of the lake for longer than people had been in the area.

The book had stories that went back to the time when the first settlers came to the lake. People had begun to see the creature almost immediately. The local aboriginal people even had stories of a lake demon, or as they called it, Naitaka, that had been seen eating birds and even deer.

I regretfully closed the book and left it on my bed. There would be plenty of time to finish my reading. Right now, Mom and I had guests.

I trotted down the stairs, leaving Krypto snoozing in the sun.

I heard Mom talking from the kitchen and went directly there. Cynthia, Mom and a lady who had to be Cynthia's mother were all seated around the table. The feelings I felt coming from the room were warm and comfortable. A lot like I would imagine Krypto's sunbeam to feel like.

"There you are, Mik," Mom said as I entered the room. "I was just about to call you again."

"Sorry, Mom. I was reading and got really caught up in the book."

Cynthia smiled a tight, formal smile at me then and her mother turned to face me. Cynthia's mom had brown hair that grew down to her shoulders and she had glasses. She wore a light blue dress that had a bird pattern to it and she looked like she was Mom's age (not that I could really tell and I wasn't about to ask).

She smiled at me too, her smile an echo of Cynthia's. "Hello, Mik. I'm Cynthia's mom, Mrs. Deets."

Mrs. Deets. I knew most adults by their first name, but I also knew some grown-ups preferred to be more formal. Mom and Dad had prepared me for that. "Hello, Mrs. Deets. I am very pleased to meet you," I said, using my best behavior. "Thank you for joining us for lunch today."

"Such fine manners!" Mrs. Deets declared and Mom beamed. "Thank you for inviting us, Mik. Cynthia and I are delighted to be here."

She turned away from me then and continued to converse with my mother.

"Mik, why don't you show Cynthia around while we ladies talk, please?" Mom said when the conversation lulled. "Lunch will ready in about thirty minutes."

"Okay, Mom," I said.

Cynthia looked at her mother. "May I go, Mother?"

"Yes, dear. But mind you stay away from the lake," Mrs. Deets said. Her tone was severe. I could almost picture her waggling her finger at Cynthia when she said it. Oddly, a flash of fear from the woman accompanied her words.

"I will, Mother," Cynthia said as she got up from the table.

We started the tour outside the cabin. Cynthia didn't speak until we were outside.

"You're lucky," were the first words she said to me.

"What do you mean," I asked.

Cynthia sat down on the porch and stared out at the lake, her shoulders rounded. She sighed. "Your mom trusts you and lets you do what you like."

"What do you mean?" Cynthia's mood was clearly going from happy to unhappy. I didn't need special powers to know that.

"If I were at home, my mother wouldn't even let me come outside by myself. She would make me stay in our cabin until she or my father were ready to go outside."

That sounded odd. "How come?"

Cynthia didn't answer me for several seconds. She went to sit on the grass and plucked a dandelion before she spoke again. "She thinks that if I go outside by myself I'll drown in the lake."

"And would you?" I asked without thinking.

Cynthia gave me one of those looks that basically says, *are you stupid*? "No! Why would I drown just by going outside?"

"I don't know. Why would your mom think that way?"

Cynthia shrugged. "I have no idea. She's always been freaked out about water. I can't even take a bath without her or Father being in the room."

"That's weird," was all I could think to say.

Cynthia changed the subject then. "Did those raccoons you were trying to stop come back?"

"They did. Do you want to see?" I helped her to her feet.

We ran around the cabin to where I had nailed the grass down again. I pointed out the pieces I had just worked on that morning. "They only rolled up a couple pieces of grass last night. I nailed them down extra hard this morning."

Cynthia looked puzzled. "But why do they roll the grass up at all?"

"They were rolling up the grass to get at the worms underneath," I said. "I actually saw a raccoon roll the grass and then dig up and eat two worms."

"Worms? Ug!" Cynthia said. "But, why would they find worms under the grass?"

"I think it's like when you pick up a rock and find worms

under it. They come up to where they are near the top of the ground but are still covered and feeling safe."

"You find worms under rocks?" Cynthia asked.

Who didn't know you could find worms under rocks? "Yes. I thought everyone knew that."

"Not me," Cynthia said. Her voice was a little sad. "Like I told you, I don't get to go outside by myself. And Father doesn't take me out to the woods to show me the stuff you are talking about."

"Too bad," I said. I meant it too. Girls are people too. They should get to learn the same stuff boys do.

"Mik! Lunch time!" Mom called from the cabin.

"Coming, Mom!" I called back. I looked at Cynthia. "Tell you what, if your parents will let me, I'll show you some of the stuff I know. Maybe we can go exploring together."

That got Cynthia's attention. I could feel excitement radiate from her. In fact, I felt more excitement than I would have ever expected.

"Is that okay, Cynthia? We could do something else if you don't want to explore."

Cynthia smiled then. "No, Mik. I would love to go exploring with you. I've never gone exploring before."

"If you're sure," I said. "I don't want you just agreeing to go cause I suggested it."

Cynthia's face lit up into a real, genuine smile. She threw her arms around me. "Don't worry about that, Mik. Thank you, I appreciate your consideration."

A girl hugging me who was not my mom. What would the guys think? "Um, sure. No problem," I said, gently disengaging myself. "We should go have lunch."

Chapter 16

Lunch with Cynthia and her mother was extremely uncomfortable. It wasn't that Mrs. Deets was mean or anything. She and my mother chatted throughout the meal, sharing stories and laughter.

No, the discomfort came from Cynthia. My new friend spent the entire meal sitting stiffly at the table, worried she would behave in a way her mother didn't approve.

I like to eat lunch quickly so Krypto and I can get outside and on with our day. Cynthia made sure she cut each morsel of food and chewed it slowly and precisely before moving onto the next.

It was like watching a robotic eating machine at work.

And, the worst part was, I didn't feel right leaving the table without Cynthia. That is, if my mother would have allowed that to happen at all. From the warning looks she shot my way accompanied by feelings of *don't you dare*, I knew I would be pressing my luck to try.

So, I slowed down my normal eating pace and tried to participate in what, I assumed, was polite adult lunch conversation.

"Mik, your mother tells me you are interested in science," Mrs. Deets said to me at one point in the meal.

"Yes, Mrs. Deets, I am," I replied. She wasn't really exhibiting any feelings of interest when she asked the question, so I wasn't sure how much to say.

"How lovely," she said, still not showing much interest.

"Yes, Mik and some of his friends did a report on Dr. Hubert Gough. It did very well," Mom said. It felt great to me that I could feel her pride behind the words.

"I'm sorry, Mildred. I'm not familiar with the name."

"Mik, could you tell Mrs. Deets who Dr. Gough is, please?"

"Sure, Mom." I mentally arranged my notes on the good doctor and began my lecture. "Dr. Hubert Gough is one of the world's foremost experts on Naitaka which is a native word that means water serpent. He is well-known for his search for the Loch Ness monster in Scotland."

"Really?" Mrs. Deets actually sounded impressed. "How very interesting."

"Yes," Mom said. "And even more interesting is the fact Dr. Gough came by our cabin the other day to say hello to Mik and me. Apparently, there is legend of a similar creature in this lake. Dr. Gough is here to investigate."

"Cool!" Cynthia said, momentarily losing her stiff composure.

"I know," I said. "I was amazed when he showed up. He even invited Mom, Dad and me to visit his camp next weekend."

"Wow," Cynthia said. "That would sure be neat to see." I could feel the slightest tinge of jealousy coming from my friend. I knew what it felt like to be left out of stuff.

"That's very interesting, Mik," said Mrs. Deets. "And will you be going along as well, Mildred?"

"Oh yes, of course. I'm quite interested to see what a scientific expedition looks like. I wouldn't miss this opportunity."

That seemed to satisfy Mrs. Deets and the conversation moved onto other things. I noticed Cynthia began to eat faster.

Cynthia and I were finished our lunch long before our mothers. I looked at my new friend and nodded toward the door. She shrugged and nodded slightly.

"Mom. Is it okay if Cynthia and I be excused to go outside to do some exploring?"

Mom, who had just been about to drink some of her coffee, set the cup down and looked at me. "Just where are you planning on going to do this exploring?"

"I hadn't really thought too much about it. Just around, I guess."

"As long as you take Krypto, it's all right with me," Mom said. She looked at Cynthia's mother. "Krypto is very intelligent, Alice. He has helped Mik several times in the past so I'm confident they will be okay. Do you have any objections?"

Cynthia's mother considered the question. I felt a spike of fear come from her as soon as I suggested Cynthia and I go out. That alone convinced me she would say *No*.

"I...guess...it would be all right," she said. The fear intensified as she spoke. There was also an undercurrent of something else. Embarrassment, maybe? "But only if Krypto goes along and you two promise me you will stay away from the water!" Her voice, while quivering a little, was still very firm.

Cynthia, who had been looking very somber, brightened up at that. "Really? Oh thank you, Mother! I promise we will stay far away from the water." She was practically bouncing as she spoke.

Mom looked at me and I knew she was waiting for my promise too. "Of course Krypto will come along. He is my best pal! I wouldn't think of going anywhere without him."

"And you will stay away from the water?" Mom asked.

"You bet!"

Mom stared at me for a moment. I felt like I was being judged.

"Very well then," Mom said. "You two may go exploring. But I want you back in an hour."

"An hour—" I began to protest, but Cynthia grabbed my hand and hauled me away from the kitchen.

"No problem, Mrs. Murdoch," she said, before I could utter another word. "We'll be back in an hour and stay far away from any water."

Before I knew it, we were out of the house and racing toward the trees, going away from the lake. We didn't stop until the trees hid us from the house.

"What the heck was that about?" I asked, when I had caught my breath.

Cynthia's smile was a little sickly. "Sorry about that, Mik. I was afraid if you said too much my mother would change her mind. She NEVER lets me go outside exploring. Not ever."

"Not ever?" That made me feel a little queasy. I couldn't imagine what life would be like if I wasn't allowed to go exploring and spend time outside with Krypto. "How come?"

"Promise you won't tell?" Cynthia asked. She looked closely at me. Both her expression and her emotions made it very clear she was serious.

What could I do? I didn't want her to stop talking to me and I was curious. "I promise."

Cynthia stared at me for a few more moments before she spoke again. "Okay, I'll tell you then. But if you blab, I'll never speak to you again."

"Who am I going to tell?" I asked. "We're out in the middle of nowhere."

"Fine!" Cynthia said. She looked around and sat down on a fallen log.

I sat down beside her. "Why do I get the feeling this is going to be a long story?"

"Don't be mean. I just wanted to sit down," Cynthia said. Her emotions had changed from serious to sad.

"I'm sorry," I said quickly. I didn't want her sad and I certainly didn't want her to cry. I wasn't sure I could handle a crying girl.

"Well, it's serious," Cynthia said. "I don't want you making fun."

"So, what is it? Why is your mother so afraid to let you go outside by yourself?"

"Well, I don't know exactly what happened," Cynthia began. "When I was very little, I fell into a swimming pool. Mom was talking to someone on the telephone and left me alone."

Her story was odd. I would have expected some sort of emotion to come from her as she told it, but there was nothing. It was like she was reciting someone else's memory. "You remember falling into a swimming pool?" I asked. "Could you swim? What was it like? Were you scared?"

Cynthia shook her head. "I don't remember anything about it, but my father told me once after it happened mother had a crying fit when I wanted to go swimming.

One moment I brought a permission slip from school and next she had collapsed on the floor and was crying uncontrollably. Father gave her a pill and put her to bed. He told me the story then."

"So, what happened?" I asked, horrified, but fascinated at the same time.

"When mother woke up, she was fine," Cynthia said.

"No, not that! What happened when you fell in the pool?"

"Well...." Cynthia gulped. "Father said Mother found me floating in the pool. He said she thought I was dead. Mother can't swim so she had to run to the neighbour's for help. They called 911 after pulling me out of the pool." Despite the seriousness of the story, Cynthia still wasn't feeling anything.

"But, everything turned out okay, right?" I said. "I mean, here you are."

Cynthia's smile was sad and she let her first emotions escape. They weren't what I expected. "I'm okay but Mother won't let me out of her sight"

"I'll bet that's frustrating," I said. "You being held back because of something you don't even remember."

Cynthia gave me a very odd look. "Mik, that's exactly how it feels. How did you know?"

I shrugged and chose my next words carefully. I didn't want to reveal my super power. "I don't know. I guess that is how I would feel if it were me."

Cynthia's smile didn't reach her eyes. "Thank you for understanding and not making fun of me, Mik. I'm actually amazed we were allowed to come outside at all."

"Well, let's not waste any time then," I said. "We had an hour, but now we only have about forty-five minutes. Let's see what we can find."

Cynthia stood and smoothed her dress. "I don't care if we find anything. I'm just glad to be outside on my own."

"Well come on! I haven't had any chance to check out the woods since we got here." I grabbed her hand and started pulling her along.

The trees weren't thick this close to the edge of the forest, but as we walked, they got closer and closer together. The trees got smaller and smaller becoming almost a thick brush. Several times we came to a spot that was impassible and had to retrace our steps to find another route.

"Phew! It's harder going than I expected," I said. "I don't think I've ever seen forest quite so thickly overgrown. There's definitely nothing like this at home."

"You know where we are, right?" Cynthia's voice shook as she spoke. "I mean, we aren't lost or anything, are we?"

I looked down at Krypto who was busy sniffing everything around us, his tail wagging. "Nah. Krypto can find our way out if I'm ever unsure. Besides, I have a pretty good sense of...."

My words were interrupted by a crashing sound further in the trees. I searched for the source, but I couldn't see anything.

The crashing continued.

Krypto had gone very still as soon as the sounds had started.

There was a long mournful bellow. It sounded like a cross between a mooing cow and the howl of a coyote at night.

It sent chills up and down my spine and Cynthia's grabbed my hand very, *very* hard.

Krypto was off, running as fast as he could, barking at whatever was out in the trees. I was about to follow, but Cynthia's grip, terrified emotions and expression of horror stopped me.

"Mik...Mik what was that? Is it a bear? Is it a cougar? Is it a wolf?"

"Cynthia, I don't have any idea. Dad said there aren't any bears, cougars or wolves around here, so probably none of those. All I know is Krypto might get into trouble. Come on, let's try to stop him!"

Cynthia looked at me with big teary, frightened eyes. She took a deep breath and nodded.

Hand-in-hand, we ran after Krypto.

Chapter 17

It wasn't hard to follow Krypto. The crashing sounds were continuing and he was barking and yelping like crazy. I was worried about him stopping, to be honest. It had happened once before when the town was being terrorized by a glowing turkey monster. Krypto had disappeared when we were investigating the creature. I thought he was eaten but it turned out he was kidnapped by the men who were posing as the beast. It took me some time to find Krypto and ultimately rescue him. For several days I didn't even know if he was alive or not. Those were some of the worst days of my life.

I wasn't about to let it happen again. As long as I could hear Krypto, I could find him.

As we ran, I tried to reach out with my mind to feel his thoughts. Make sure he was all right. The problem was, I was holding Cynthia's hand and her feelings were drowning out everything else. She was scared. Really scared, just like me.

"It's going to be okay, Cynthia," I said as I ran. I wasn't sure I believed what I was saying, but I had to do something to calm her fears.

Cynthia didn't even slow down. "Do you really think so?" She was gasping a little as she spoke. I guess that being stuck in the house with her mother all day meant she didn't get as much exercise as Krypto and I normally did. I wasn't tired at all.

We kept running and the trees got thicker. Krypto's barking was getting closer and the sounds of crashing had stopped. I hoped that meant whatever Krypto was barking at had decided to leave.

We practically had to shove our way through the last stand of trees and bushes before we found Krypto. He was jumping up and down, barking at an almost impenetrable wall of small brush. The trees nearest to him were scratched and scarred from his toenails, showing just how hard he had been trying to break through.

"Okay, Cynthia. I'm going to try and grab Krypto. You stand back because he's pretty excited and I don't want him to accidentally bite or scratch you."

Cynthia nodded and stood back to watch me.

I whistled softly. "Okay, Krypto. I'm here. Come on boy. Let's leave whatever is on the other side of these trees alone." I tried to enhance the soothing sound of my voice by projecting thoughts of peace toward him as I spoke.

Krypto stopped jumping and looked at me, his tongue lolling. He whined and looked at the line of trees then back at me. It was clear he wanted me to come closer and help him investigate whatever had caught his attention.

I shook my head at him. "Not right now, buddy. Whatever that thing is, it doesn't want us around. We need to turn around and go back home." I crept up to him as I spoke, still radiating feelings of peace and quiet. When I was close enough, I grabbed his collar.

At my touch, Krypto almost went boneless, collapsing to the ground, fast asleep. That was when I realized how hard I had been projecting my emotions. The poor guy never had a chance when I touched him. I had no idea my power worked that way or was even that strong. I was going to have to be careful in the future. Krypto was still breathing but was he all right? I had no idea.

As he went limp, I heard a squeak from the direction of Cynthia. "Is...is he all right? Why did he fall down?"

I had to play dumb then, even though I was freaked out about Krypto. After all, I didn't want Cynthia to know about my super power. "I don't know. Maybe he was over-excited and fainted when we found him."

"Fainted? A dog?" Cynthia didn't look convinced. "That doesn't happen. Is he okay?"

I shrugged, still trying to maintain the charade of innocence. "I don't know what's going on. Krypto is still breathing, so I hope he's all right."

"I don't know...." Cynthia began to say.

She was interrupted by a moaning cough that came from beyond the line of trees. Not only beyond, but several feet above the ground. That convinced me that maybe Dad was wrong and it really was some sort of cougar. I looked as hard as I could for the cat, but I could see nothing.

I picked up Krypto, who slept on, and began backing away and casting my thoughts out, trying to catch any emotions. I really hoped my friend *really* was asleep. Krypto is only about the size of a cocker spaniel but I knew even his small size would get heavy quickly.

I cast my mind out, searching for any emotions. The only thing I could feel was anger overlaid with curiosity.

The sound of crashing started again, but only for a moment. It was replaced by splashing. Water nearby?

I kept focused on the feeling of curiosity. It was being

replaced by something else. Something I couldn't quite figure out. All I knew was, the emotions were coming from the same place.

I started walking to follow the source of those feelings, somehow managing to keep from smacking into trees.

"Where are you going?" Cynthia asked, following me.

"I'm trying to find out what's on the other side of these trees," I said, not stopping.

"Why?" Cynthia asked. "Don't you think that could be dangerous?"

"It could," I admitted. "But, if Krypto was willing to come chasing after it once, he might again. Next time, I might not be around to stop him. I want to know if I need to start walking him on a leash."

"That makes sense," Cynthia said. She followed me in silence then.

The trees weren't getting any thinner but the ground was definitely getting wetter. Leaf litter and dirt were replaced with a spongy, mossy ground cover that oozed water. A couple times I caught a glimpse of water through small gaps in the trees. All the while, I followed the feelings of something. I still didn't know what. I was pretty sure it wasn't human, whatever it was.

And then, the feelings were gone like the thing had never existed.

I just stopped then, confused by the change. Now what? That's when I noticed how tired my arms were from the weight of my pal.

I looked at Cynthia. She looked at me.

"Why did you stop, Mik?" Cynthia asked.

"I...don't know," I said. "I can't hear anything on the other side of the trees. I was at least hearing some splashing before, but now there's nothing. And besides, my arms are killing me." I lay Krypto down on a dry patch of ground and massaged my aching arms.

"So, what are we going to do?"

I looked back the way we had come and then the other direction. I shrugged. "I don't know if turning back is going to help us. We should probably just go back to the cabin now."

Cynthia's expression changed from one of concern to relief. "I'm glad to hear you say that, Mik. I don't want to go back into the forest right now. I'm scared of whatever that thing is."

I realized then I had been selfish. Being a superhero, I'm used to weird stuff. I hadn't even considered how Cynthia might feel about tracking down a mystery creature. I looked at her. "I'm really sorry, Cynthia. I should have asked you if you wanted to follow the creature."

Cynthia smiled then. "I know you want to protect your dog. I understand that, so I didn't want to stop you from searching."

Krypto let out a soft snore then and Cynthia giggled. "I wouldn't want anything to happen to Krypto either."

I grinned. "I think Krypto is having the best part of this little adventure. He got some exercise and now...." I looked down at him. "...and now he is getting a snooze and a free ride."

"Do you know where we are, now?" Cynthia asked, looking a little worried.

I looked up at the sky and saw the sun was lower back the way we had come. "Not for sure, but I know we went west from the cabin and the sun sets to the west, which is that way." I pointed back where we had been.

"So, we keep going this way and we should get to the lake?" Cynthia asked, nodding her head the way we had been walking.

"I think so," I said.

"What are we waiting for?" Cynthia asked, taking the lead for the first time. "Let's get going."

I picked up Krypto and trailed after her.

Chapter 18

I followed Cynthia through the woods, still carrying Krypto. Despite being bumped and shaken he still showed no signs of waking up. I was beginning to worry, to be honest. I mean, what kind of dog just falls over in a deep sleep for no apparent reason? Cynthia hadn't really said much, but I could see her look at us from the corner of her eyes every few minutes. The strongest feeling I could gain from her was curiosity.

From Krypto? Well, I was pretty sure he was having some happy dreams. Occasionally he would twitch and whine, but that was it. That and steady breathing.

What was I going to do?

"Does he do that often?" Cynthia finally asked. She had stopped to wait for me to catch up.

By this point, Krypto had been sleeping on the ground and in my arms for about fifteen minutes as near as I could figure it.

I took the opportunity to rest. I sat down with him still in my arms. I shook my head. "No. This is the first time."

"Weird," was all Cynthia said.

"Yup."

"So, where do you think we are?" Cynthia asked when she realized I wasn't going to say anything more.

I shrugged. "Closer to the lake. It shouldn't be long now."

"What are you going to do with your dog when we get out of the forest?"

I considered that question for a moment before answering. "I'm going to try and wake Krypto up." Even as I said the words, I wondered what I could possibly do. I considered sending more strong emotions his way, but what emotion would wake a sleeping dog? I guess I could try fear, but I didn't want to scare my pal to death.

Cynthia's next question echoed my thoughts. "How are you going to do that? He doesn't seem to want to wake up even though he's getting shaken and we are being pretty noisy."

"Water maybe," I said. "I know I've seen sleeping people wake up when they get soaked with cold water."

"That might work. Are you ready to keep going?"

I nodded and climbed to my feet. "Thanks for the break. Krypto is heavier than he looks."

Cynthia smiled and took the lead again.

My guess about being close to the lake was pretty accurate. About five minutes after our rest we came out of the thickest part of the trees. The impenetrable wall of trees we had been walking beside thinned, and the water we had originally heard turned out to be a narrow river no wider than a couple of cars end-to-end.

We kept walking.

Ten minutes after we first saw the water, we got to the bridge that crossed the river on the path between my house and Cynthia's. Whatever we had heard was somewhere back in the river or along it. The only way we would find it would be to be in or on the water, swimming or in a boat. That brush was just too thick to get through without an axe.

We stopped beside the bridge and I splashed some water on Krypto's muzzle.

Nothing.

I dipped the tip of his tail into the water. That didn't do any good either.

Cynthia, who had been watching my attempts, spoke up. "Why don't you just throw him into the water? It's not very deep here." There was something a little odd about the way she asked the question. Almost like she was afraid that I would do exactly as she asked.

I shook my head. "No. If I were to throw him in and he doesn't wake up, he would drown or I would get very wet rescuing him."

Cynthia looked relieved to hear that. "That's good. Why don't you splash more of him with water? It shouldn't hurt him, right?"

I really had nothing to lose at that point. I lay Krypto beside the water and starting splashing him. As I splashed I threw thoughts of the raccoons toward him. I knew that thoughts of raccoons weren't the same as emotions, but I had to try.

I probably splashed water on him for a good thirty seconds before his eyes fluttered open. Of course, he saw me splashing him.

Krypto climbed to his feet and shook himself, looking at me reproachfully. I could almost hear him asking me what I thought I was doing.

I didn't care. He was awake and okay.

Cynthia clapped her hands with a small laugh. "I'm so glad he's awake. But we should get back to your house. I'm sure my mother is wondering where we are."

Chapter 19

That night I dreamed about the raccoons again. Just like before, the dream was so vivid it woke me from a deep sleep and just like before, it happened in the middle of the night.

As soon as I woke up, I knew something was happening. The raw, mischievous and curious emotions that I had come to associate with the masked creatures was front and centre in my mind. Somehow, their presence automatically triggered dreams about them like some weird alarm.

I pulled my slippers and robe on and went to my window to listen.

Sure enough, there was the tell-tale banging of cans. Cans that I knew only too well had to be our garbage. I had put them out for the garbage-men to pick up in the morning. I could only assume that the masked marauders found them first.

I rushed down the stairs and out the front door, a plan forming in my mind as I ran. I had already proven I could frighten and even put Krypto to sleep with a blast of emotion. I wasn't about to try and touch the raccoons to put them to sleep, but maybe I could scare them away.

But what would a raccoon be afraid of?

That's when I remembered the movie *Over the Hedge*. The raccoon in that story was deathly afraid of a big bear.

I'll be honest, I have no idea how a bear thinks or feels. All I could do was try to feel hungry and excited about eating raccoons. I also tried to roar like a hungry bear. I did my best to *throw* my thoughts at them.

The raccoons went very still the first time I did it but they did not run away as I had hoped. Their emotions hadn't really changed in any way. They weren't any more afraid than when I first detected them. If anything, they were more curious.

I decided to turn up the hunger emotion and throw in a touch of anger. I roared again.

This time they started moving, but not away. They were actually coming closer to me. The sense of curiosity coming from them kept growing. Somehow, I wasn't projecting well enough.

Krypto, who had come outside with me, was looking at me oddly. I could tell that he was trying to figure out what the heck I was doing. Obviously, I wasn't projecting my feelings very well because he stood right next to me and didn't seem afraid at all.

The raccoons were even closer than before. If they saw me, I knew I wouldn't have a hope of scaring them away with emotions. They would know I wasn't the bear I was pretending to be. I had one more chance.

This time, I envisioned myself as a large bear. In my thoughts I wrapped the bear persona around myself. I was hungry. I was angry and most of all, I wanted to eat pesky raccoons. I really had to make myself believe it.

Krypto started to back away from me as I worked on my bear self-image. When I roared, he yelped and ran into the house. That made me feel good and bad. I hoped I had convinced the raccoons.

Krypto's flight had momentarily distracted me from the intruders. When I felt for their emotions, they were gone. Score one for the home team.

But, would they stay away? And how much of a mess had they made?

The mess would have to wait. I could feel Krypto's fear coming from my room like a raw wave. I was pretty sure I would find him cowering under my bed. I had to make things right with him.

Ω Ω Ω

I found Krypto where I expected — under my bed. I coaxed him out and onto the foot where he normally slept. I climbed into bed myself and was soon asleep.

My sleep was uninterrupted by dreams or anything else for the rest of the night. Krypto lay shivering on my bed at my feet. Whatever I had done to the raccoons had put a real scare into him too.

I realized something was wrong as soon as I woke. Krypto was still shivering in his sleep as if he was nervous or scared...and, the foot of my bed was wet! Krypto had peed on my bed! He never did that. He hadn't made a mess in the house since he was a tiny puppy. What was going on?

He jumped off my bed as I got up, looking and feeling very guilty. He knew what he had done and was sorry. That much was obvious. At the same time, still terrified by what I had done, he sat on the floor shivering. I was certain if he realized I was the one who had done it, he wouldn't have anything to do with me.

I had to figure out how to comfort my best friend, but I didn't know how to do it. I had to give it some thought. My bed I could deal with while I was thinking. I stripped off the blankets and sheets and hung them over the furniture in my bedroom to dry. When I was done, it looked like I had been building a fort.

Then I did my morning routine and went down to the kitchen for breakfast. Mom was sitting at the table looking bleary eyed. Her hair was mussed and she was still in her robe.

I actually stared for several moments hardly believing my eyes. Mom was always up and dressed before me, wide-awake and ready for anything. This was very different for her.

"Mom?"

"Hmm?" Mom looked up at me, her hands wrapped around her coffee mug like it was the only thing keeping her alive.

"Are you okay?"

"I'm fine, Mik. Why do you ask?"

"Cause you're not dressed and you look half asleep," I said. I didn't want to tell her she looked terrible. That would hurt her feelings. But, I did need to be honest.

Mom laughed. "Yes, I suppose I do look kind of terrible." She sat up and stretched. "I guess I've been thinking of those pesky raccoons too much." She forced a laugh. "I dreamed I was one of them last night. And a bear was trying to eat me. It woke me up from a deep sleep and every time I closed my eyes, it woke me again so I'm kind of tired this morning."

I couldn't believe what I was hearing. Once again, my power had been much stronger than I expected. First putting Krypto to sleep, then freaking out my pal and now stopping my mom from sleeping.

"Are you okay, Mom?"

Mom smiled. "I'm fine, honey. Just tired. Think you can get your own breakfast today?"

"Sure, Mom! Can I get you anything too?"

"That's very thoughtful, Mik. Maybe a couple pieces of buttered toast if you don't mind?"

"You got it, Mom," I said. I got to work making Mom and me breakfast. I made toast and got out some cereal. I caught Krypto watching me from beside his bowl. He nudged it with his nose when he saw me looking. I guess hunger overruled fear. I laughed and fed him too.

The entire time I worked, my mind was racing. I hadn't given my super power much thought when I first knew I had it. Now I was coming to realize it was more powerful than I ever thought it could be. In fact, I was starting to think it could be too dangerous to use.

I mean, what if I scared someone or something so badly it died? Or maybe I put Krypto to sleep by accident and he didn't ever wake up again?

It wasn't like I could practice using it by myself. The only way to practice was if other people or creatures were around and I didn't want to hurt anybody.

I looked over at my mother who was nibbling on one of the pieces of toast. I knew she wasn't hurt, but at the same time I felt awful for keeping her awake. She was the last person I wanted to hurt. It was my job to protect her!

"Mom, I'm going to go outside."

Mom didn't even look up. "Have fun, honey."

Krypto followed me as far as the door of the house and stopped. His shivering got worse and I could feel the waves of fear and anxiety rolling off him like waves on the ocean. Krypto was too afraid of what I had done to go outside to play.

I decided then I wasn't going to use my super power

anymore. It was a brutal decision. I'd always wanted a super power but, now that I had one, I couldn't even use it. It was simply too dangerous.

I went outside, feeling like I had just thrown away my favourite toy. I was very aware Krypto, my best friend and constant companion, was not walking beside me. It felt like a part of me was missing.

I sighed then and looked around the yard. Better check to see what the raccoons had done.

Ω Ω Ω

I almost changed my mind about using my powers when I saw the devastation caused by the raccoons. The unwanted marauders had knocked over and opened every one of the garbage cans and trash was scattered everywhere.

I started picking up the garbage, wondering how they had managed to get them open. I had used carabineers to fasten the lids closed. It hadn't been enough.

I kept picking up trash.

"Hey, Mik, what happened?"

I jumped at the sound of Cynthia's voice. I had been so focused on cleaning up that I hadn't heard or felt her coming.

That suited me just fine.

"Hey, Cynthia. The raccoons were back last night. As you can see, they made a real mess."

"At least they didn't roll up the grass again."

"Really?" In my hurry to check the garbage cans, I hadn't even looked. "I guess that's something." I felt a little better knowing the grass was finally getting a chance.

Cynthia looked around. "Where's Krypto? He isn't sleeping again, is he?"

My momentary good mood came crashing down. "He's in the house." My voice was quiet and low when I spoke.

"How come? Is something wrong?" I felt Cynthia's curiosity then. That made it worse.

"He's afraid to come outside," I said. I felt terrible saying that.

Cynthia's curiosity intensified. "Afraid to come outside? That doesn't sound like Krypto. What's he afraid of?"

Should I tell her? It was starting to eat at me. Would she even believe me if I told her? Could I trust Cynthia? The more I thought about it the more I knew I had to talk to someone. I just didn't know how much I could safely say.

Chapter 20

"I scared him," I said quietly.

Cynthia leaned close to me. "I'm sorry, Mik. I didn't quite hear you."

I swallowed. "I said, I scared him." No sense lying about it. Nothing good ever came from lies. I felt a little better with my admission.

Cynthia looked puzzled and shook her head. "I don't understand. What could you have done that would have scared Krypto so much that he won't come out of the house? He was fine yesterday, wasn't he? Other than falling asleep, that is."

I shook my head, feeling miserable again. "No, he was fine when we got home. In fact he was fine right up until the raccoons came."

"Mik, you're not making much sense," Cynthia said. "Whatever happened, we can fix it."

I wished I could believe her. I shrugged.

"So, what happened?" Cynthia asked again. "I can't help if I don't know what happened."

What to tell her? "I'm not sure you will believe me," I said.

"You won't know if you never tell me," Cynthia said. I could tell she was starting to get frustrated.

I turned and faced her directly, taking a deep breath. "Fine! I'll tell you the truth. You won't believe it, but what I'm about to say is true. All of it." I watched her for a moment. She nodded.

I took another deep breath. "Cynthia, I have...." I caught myself and thought about what I was about to do. I really didn't know Cynthia all that well and telling her about my power to feel and send emotions could put her in danger.

"Mik?"

I decided then. I had already frightened Krypto. I didn't have the right to put Cynthia in danger or scare her too.

I shook my head. "Nothing, Cynthia. Krypto's frightened, is all. Maybe it was the creature we heard in the woods yesterday or maybe he smelled something. I don't know."

"That's not what you were going to say," Cynthia said. Her emotions spiked then, from frustrated to angry.

I shrugged. There wasn't anything I could say.

"If that's the way you want it!" Cynthia turned from me then and started to stomp away. She was almost out of the yard when she turned and faced me. "I thought you were different. I thought you were my friend!" I saw the tears in her eyes before she left. I could sense the feelings of hurt and betrayal from her.

I sat down on the grass amongst the trash and hung my head, not knowing what to do next. In less than a day I scared my best friend so badly he wouldn't leave the house, kept my mother from sleeping and making her feel unwell *and* I made the only person my age at the lake mad at me. Probably mad enough she would never speak to me again.

It's one thing to read in a comic book how super powers can make a person's life difficult. It was something totally different having it happen.

"Mik!" I heard Mom call me from the front porch.

"Coming, Mom," I called back. Her voice sounded urgent. What else could go wrong?

Ω Ω Ω

I found Mom up in my room.

"Mik, why is your bed torn apart?" she asked when she saw me.

"I'm drying out the sheets and blanket," I searched my mind trying to remember if I had closed the door to my room or not.

Mom gave me a stern look. "Why are your sheets and blanket wet?"

"Well...Krypto was frightened last night and slept on the foot of the bed. Some time last night he had an accident."

"Krypto had an accident on your bed? Honey, you can't just dry out the sheets and sleep in dried dog pee. It isn't healthy."

"I'm sorry, Mom. I didn't want Krypto to get into trouble and I didn't think it through. I also didn't want to make any more work for you."

Mom smiled. "That's okay, Mik. Now you know." She started gathering the bedding. "That reminds me...have you noticed anything odd about Krypto's behaviour? He hasn't left the house all day."

I felt more miserable than ever. "I think whatever scared Krypto last night is why, Mom."

"Scared of raccoons?" I could feel her doubt radiating from her mind. "That doesn't sound like our Krypto. Maybe he isn't feeling well."

I shrugged. I couldn't tell her the real reason he was afraid. Firstly, she wouldn't believe me and even worse, if she did, my super hero career would be over. I wished I knew how to make Krypto better. I wished I had someone to talk to.

As that last thought passed through my mind, I couldn't help but think of Cynthia and how she was now angry with me. I mentally kicked myself. I had someone my age to talk to who wanted to be my friend and I pushed her away. My super power secret would be safe with her because she didn't even live in my town.

Mom bundled up the sheets. "We need to watch Krypto and make sure he is all right. Please ensure he is eating and drinking properly. If he isn't, we will have to take him into the vet for a check-up."

"Okay, Mom," I said. Her suggestion was completely logical and would give me some time to try and come up with a plan to help Krypto overcome his fear.

It might even give me time to figure out how to talk to Cynthia again.

Ω Ω Ω

Cynthia and her mom were supposed to come over to our house for lunch. Cynthia's mom called about half an hour before they were supposed to arrive. Cynthia wasn't feeling well and they weren't coming. I knew the truth. It wasn't that Cynthia was sick, it was that she was angry with me.

That made me feel even worse. Now Mom was going to be without her daily visit and it was my fault. What was I going to do? I could have asked Mom, but she would have peppered me with lots of questions I didn't want to answer. Things like, *What did you do to Cynthia? Why is Cynthia mad at you?* I knew what she would tell me to do, too. *Go over to Cynthia's house and apologize.*

Don't think that idea hadn't crossed my mind. But, the problem with apologizing was, once I did it, Cynthia would ask again about why Krypto was scared and I still wasn't ready to tell her my secret. I wasn't sure I ever would be. Revealing your secret identity wasn't something done without a great deal of thought. When I refused to answer the question, she would be mad again and I would have to start all over.

And I knew the second try would be that much harder.

There was a problem I could try to deal with closer to home though. Krypto was still huddled in the house, alternating between napping and hiding. In both cases, he was almost continuously shivering from fear.

I sat down beside him during one of his many naps. The poor little guy was scared, even while he was asleep. I could feel it. And I could hear his occasional whimpering and see the twitching of his feet while he ran away in his dreams.

I thought about what I'd done to frighten the raccoons, and by accident, Krypto.

I had tried several things, but the final image I had projected along with the feelings was that of a giant, hungry bear. The image of the bear had done the trick.

I didn't think Krypto had ever seen a bear before. Obviously, the image I had projected was strong enough that it hadn't mattered. The raccoons had scampered away into the night and my dog was traumatized.

I scratched behind Krypto's ears as he slept and I could feel his fear ease a little. I hoped it was because he knew I was with him and he was safe.

It didn't fix the problem though.

Maybe if I softened the bear a little. Made the projected feelings and image less scary, it would help Krypto.

156

There was no time like the present, so I gently shook my pal and called his name. "Krypto!"

It took almost a minute, but he woke and looked at me through sleepy eyes.

"Sorry to wake you, Krypto, but I have an idea that might make you feel better."

His tail thumped a few times in a half-awake attempt to wag.

I leaned close to him and looked him right in the eyes. I projected the less threatening image of the bear along with feelings of friendship toward Krypto with my mind.

Krypto let out a yelp and was out of the room before I could react. He ran directly upstairs to hide.

It took me more than ten minutes to find him under some laundry, his shaking worse than before. I sat down beside him, scooped him onto my lap and started petting and talking softly to him. It took me a long time to calm him enough that he was able to sleep again.

That was an epic fail! I only managed to make things worse.

I got up and carried him downstairs and put him into his bed. I covered him with a blanket and left the house for a walk.

I went down to the lake and was surprised to find Mom sitting on a lawn chair looking out over the water.

"Hi, Mom. What are you doing here?"

"Oh, hello, Mik," Mom said, looking over her shoulder at me. "I'm just enjoying the lake since we don't have any company."

"Oh," I said. "Sorry."

Mom straightened a little and looked more closely at me.

"Why would you be sorry? It's not your fault they aren't here. Cynthia is sick. That's all. There will be other days."

"I guess I'm sorry that you are stuck here without any company," I said. "I know you enjoy visiting with Mrs. Deets."

"Mik, you are all the company I need," Mom said gently. "You are right though. I do enjoy Alice's company. But I like being alone sometimes too."

"Oh," I said again. I looked out at the lake. It looked so peaceful; it was hard to believe that something could be lurking beneath the waves.

Chapter 21

We walked over to Cynthia's house the next day. Naturally, Krypto stayed home. He still wouldn't go outside except to scamper in and out to go to the bathroom, and even that reluctantly.

Mrs. Deets met us at the door. "Thank you for coming over Mildred. I missed our chat yesterday."

"I did too," Mom said. "How is Cynthia feeling?"

"Oh, that girl!" Mrs. Deets said. "She won't come out of her room or take anything. I'm not sure she's really sick at all but she won't tell me what's wrong."

"Mik could try to talk to her," Mom suggested.

I felt like I was being offered to the lions with that comment. I knew I had to talk to Cynthia, but to be volunteered? "Yeah, sure," I said, trying to sound upbeat.

"Would you, Mik?" Mrs. Deets asked. I could feel her relief and hope. "I'm practically at my wits end. Cynthia can be moody sometimes and I'm never sure what will bring her out."

"I would be happy to," I said, my heart sinking further. I knew what was bothering her, but telling both mothers would only raise unwanted questions. Secret identities could be such a pain sometimes. "Where is Cynthia?"

"She should be up in her room," Mrs. Deets said.

"Okay. I'll go see her now," I said, turning toward the stairs that led up to Cynthia's bedroom.

"Will you let me know what you find out?" Mrs. Deets asked.

I shrugged. "I'll try. I've got to find out what's wrong first. Cynthia may not even talk to me."

Mrs. Deets smiled then. "Cynthia will talk to you. She said you are her friend."

That surprised me. Cynthia considered me a friend? That might actually explain why she was so upset with me. She thought I was her friend, but I didn't return the favour.

I went up to her room and softly knocked on the door. "Cynthia?"

"Go away!" Her voice was muffled by the door a little, but the barrier didn't stop the wave of sorrow that she was feeling from slamming into my brain.

"Cynthia, I'm sorry I made you sad," I said. "Please. Will you talk to me?"

"Why should I?" Sorrow was replaced, a little at least, by curiosity and suspicion.

"Your mother is worried about you." I knew as soon as I spoke the words, it was the wrong thing to say.

"Go away, Mik! I don't want to talk to you or anybody." Cynthia's emotions were suddenly closed to me. It was like a door had closed in my mind. I couldn't sense what she was feeling at all. Now what?

I sighed. I hadn't realized how much my little slip had hurt Cynthia's feelings. What could I say to fix this? Could I trust her with my secret? Maybe a better question was: should I tell her?

I realized then, in a rare flash of insight, that telling her my secret might be the only way to fix our friendship.

As I thought about us as friends, I knew it was true. I liked Cynthia. In the brief time we had known each other I had felt very comfortable talking to her. That was odd because I hadn't had much luck with girls. I thought about my run in with a girl and her dog back home after I first decided to become a superhero. The girl, Lillian, had made my life miserable getting me suspended from school for the injury of a teacher. An injury that Lillian had caused.

Did I want to lose the one friend I had at the lake? The only female friend my age I'd ever really had?

I decided I didn't want to lose Cynthia's friendship.

"Cynthia?"

"I told you to go away!" she said from beyond the door.

"I can't do that. You're my friend and you are sad," I said. "I know I'm the cause and I'm sorry. Not because your mother wants to know what's wrong but because I like you and want to keep being your friend."

I waited then, trying to give Cynthia time to decide what to do. Her emotions were still closed to me, which I found very uncomfortable. I hadn't realized until that moment how much I was starting to depend on knowing what other people were feeling. It was weird not to sense them now.

"Mik?"

"I'm still here," I said. "I told you, I'm not going anywhere.

"Oh, fine!" Cynthia said. Her voice was much closer to the

door. "You might as well come in." The door opened and Cynthia looked out at me. Her eyes were red and swollen from crying.

"I'm sorry," I said simply.

"Why are you here?" Cynthia asked as I walked into her room.

"We came over to visit," I said. "Remember, our mothers talk nearly every day. We did too for a while."

"Until you didn't trust me," Cynthia said, her voice bitter.

"You don't understand," I said. "Close the door and I'll try to explain."

Cynthia closed the door and we sat on the bed, facing each other. "Before I tell you my secret, you have to swear you won't tell anyone. Not your mom or dad. Not even your best friend."

Cynthia's laugh held no humour. "No problem there, Mik. Mom, Dad and I don't talk about anything that matters and you are my only friend."

That shocked me. I always went to my parents with anything that bothered me and we'd discuss big things as a family. It never occurred to me other families were different.

And I was her only friend? I wasn't the most popular kid around, but even I had a few friends. To have none at all? I couldn't even imagine that.

"Really, Cynthia. That's awful," I said. I looked around then, almost like I was making sure no one else was listening.

"What are you doing, Mik? There's no one here but you and me," Cynthia said.

"Sorry," I said. "I never expected to tell anyone this. I'm having trouble getting used to the idea."

"Tell me what?" Cynthia asked.

"My secret," I said. "I've got to warn you, it will sound pretty far-fetched. But everything I'm about to tell you is absolutely true."

Cynthia's expression was as serious as my explanation. "Okay, Mik. What is it? Are you dying or something?"

"No, nothing like that." I hesitated for a moment, searching for the right words. "You know how Krypto is acting so odd, right?" I didn't wait for any acknowledgement from Cynthia. I ploughed on. "His behavior is because of something I did to scare away the raccoons the other night."

"You mean, like how you nailed the grass down?" Cynthia asked.

"No," I said. "It's totally different. The grass was using something physical to stop the raccoons. What I did to scare them was with my mind." I was too far along to stop now, so I kept talking. "I used my mind to project the emotion of fear with the image of a large, hungry bear. The combination not only sent them running, but scared Krypto so badly he won't leave the house."

"Projected?" Cynthia was puzzled. I didn't have to sense her emotions to know that, and for some reason I still couldn't pick up anything from her. She was a closed as her door. "You mean like with a projector? A movie?"

I shook my head. "No. More like, with my thoughts. You see, and this is the part that's hard to believe, I have the ability to sense and send emotions. I used that power on the raccoons. Krypto was an unfortunate casualty."

"You have the ability to sense and send emotions?" Cynthia stood and looked over at me. "And what's that like?"

I couldn't tell if she was being serious or not. Her expression gave nothing away and, as I've already said, her emotions were hidden from me. "To tell you the truth, it was pretty weird at first. Knowing how someone is feeling is definitely an advantage and I have to be careful not to misuse it. Being able to project emotions is something I've only learned to do since I came here."

"So, how am I feeling right now?" Cynthia asked, watching me carefully.

I shrugged. "I have no idea. For some reason, while I was outside your room, your feelings suddenly disappeared. When I first got here, you were feeling absolutely wretched. Now...I don't know."

"Let's assume for a moment that I believe everything you've told me. Maybe you can't sense my feelings now because your abilities are gone."

"No," I said, shaking my head. "I can still sense the feelings of your mother and mine."

"Okay. I guess I can understand why you didn't want to tell me about the emotion-thing. It does sound pretty far-fetched."

"You're taking this awfully well. I expected you to call me a liar and throw me out of your room."

"Well, the way I see it, either you are telling the truth or you are crazy. If you're telling the truth, I want to know what I can do to help. If you're crazy, I've got to keep a close eye on you anyway to keep you from hurting yourself and others."

I had to laugh then. "Fair enough. Make sure you keep the number for the funny farm handy, just in case." I sighed then. "But, in all seriousness, I'm being totally honest with you. I got my powers from a magic berry. It was given to me by a medicine man for some of the things I've done around Cranberry Flats."

"What kinds of things?" Cynthia asked. She came and sat down again.

"Well, I stopped some guys who were dressing up as a

glowing turkey creature to try and scare people. I also tried to help a family that didn't have a place to live. I don't know, but I think those things might be why."

"That sounds pretty heroic to me," Cynthia said.

I think I blushed a little. I definitely didn't know how to respond to that. "Yes, well, I have a problem and maybe you can help. I tried to help Krypto stop being so frightened, but I think I only made it worse."

"What did you do?"

So, I told Cynthia about my last attempt. She listened intently, nodding at my words.

"I think I know what you were trying to do, but I also think I know why it didn't work," she said when I finished. "You tried to make the bear seem friendly. The problem is, Krypto is already afraid of the bear. He has no reason to believe anything has changed."

"So, what do I do?" I asked.

Cynthia looked very intently at me. "Who does Krypto trust more than anyone in the world?"

I thought about that. "Me, I suppose. And maybe Mom and Dad to a lesser degree."

"What if you changed the bear to look like you and make the emotions feel friendly instead?" Cynthia said.

"That could work, I suppose. Except, the minute Krypto gets the image of the bear, he runs for it."

"When he's awake. What if you did it while he was sleeping? It would be a bad dream for him at first, but then it would turn good and he would still be sleeping. He wouldn't leave while you were doing it and he might even wake up cured."

That sounded promising. "Maybe," I said. "But, would you help me? I still don't know if I have enough control of my powers. You might be able to see and feel what I'm projecting enough to guide me."

Cynthia gave me a hug. "I would be happy to help."

Chapter 22

It was really hard to resist trying Cynthia's plan on Krypto as soon as I got home. I wanted Krypto to be back to his old self.

Then, I saw him shivering in his basket and I knew I had to wait. The poor little guy lay buried under his blanket, not coming out. By the smell, he hadn't even left to go to the bathroom.

I cleaned him up as best I could and sat by him until he dozed off again. I knew, if things didn't change soon, Mom would send Krypto to the veterinarian. I also knew the vet wouldn't be able to do much to help my pal.

That made the waiting even harder.

I moved his basket up to my room to buy some time. I reasoned if Mom didn't see the extent of Krypto's suffering, I might have time to fix the problem.

To pass the time, I went outside exploring. I wanted to know if the raccoons were gone for good or if they had only retreated a short distance. The grass was starting to show signs of growth. It had been turning a little brown from all the times it had been rolled up but now new grass was coming up. I watered it to encourage it more.

Despite Cynthia's question about whether my power had left me or not, I knew it was getting stronger. I could sense Krypto's frightened misery from further away with every passing day. Maybe it was because we were friends or maybe it was because I expected to sense him. Whatever the reason, I knew whenever he woke up or had an accident or went back to sleep.

The raccoons, and any sign of them, were nowhere to be found.

My powers had really done the job of scaring them away.

Even that small victory felt hollow when I considered how Krypto had been harmed. I was just glad Mom wasn't complaining about nightmares anymore too.

I got back from my exploring just as Cynthia and her mother were coming down the pathway. I had known they were coming for some time; I could sense them (remember how I mentioned that my powers were getting stronger?). That included Cynthia again. I still had no idea why she had stopped registering for that short while.

"Hello, Mrs. Deets. Hi, Cynthia," I said as I saw them.

"Hi, Mik," Cynthia said with a wave. She looked much happier today. "How's Krypto?"

"The same," I said. "Do you want to come up to my room to see him?"

"Sure! May I go, Mother?"

"Of course, dear," Mrs. Deets said. "Please let your mother know I'm here, Mik."

"I will!" Cynthia and I ran ahead into the house. "Mom! Mrs. Deets is here. Cynthia and I are going upstairs."

I barely heard Mom's, "Thank you, Mik," before we were past her and up the stairs.

I opened the door to my room quietly. Krypto was huddled in his basket asleep like I knew he would be. Did I really think I could help my friend?

"Mik, what are you waiting for?" Cynthia asked when I stood watching Krypto for too long. "Aren't you going to help Krypto? Or have you already done it?"

"No, I haven't done anything yet," I said. I was waiting for you and, to tell the truth, I'm a little worried."

"What are you worried about?"

"That I won't be able to help Krypto. That I'll only make things worse."

Cynthia stood in front of me and looked me straight in the eyes. "Mik, I don't know if you can help Krypto or not, but worrying about it won't help."

"And if I make things worse?"

"Mik, is Krypto going outside by himself?" Cynthia quizzed. "It doesn't smell like it. I don't want to be mean, but your bedroom really stinks right now. Like a dog's bathroom."

"Yeah. Sorry about that," I said. I looked at my sleeping dog. "I guess you're right. He can't be much worse. I'm just so worried about him."

"I know, Mik. So the sooner you try, the sooner you will know if you have helped him." Cynthia pulled the desk chair out for me. "Here, sit down and make yourself comfortable. Then you can get going."

I sat in the chair and looked down at the sleeping dog, collecting my thoughts and visualizing what I was about to do. It was a simple enough plan. I was going to start by projecting the fear and image of the snarling bear. Then I would slowly change fear to happiness and, at the same time, change the bear's appearance from terrifying beast to me.

I took a deep breath. "I'm ready."

"Okay," said Cynthia, sitting down on my bed. "Will I be able to feel or see any of this?"

"I don't know," I admitted. "I think so. The first time I did this, I wasn't directing it at Krypto at all. Just the raccoons. He got it, just the same."

I took another deep breath and closed my eyes. Just like the first time, I projected out feelings of fear and hunger. At the same time, I tried to picture a giant black bear snarling and growling. Krypto started to whimper in his sleep.

"Yipes!" Cynthia said jumping up, her emotions suddenly spiking.

I lost my focus and the image and the emotions I had been projecting quit. Krypto stopped whimpering immediately.

"You really *can* project emotions, can't you?" she asked.

"I told you," I said. "Now, I have to start again."

"Sorry," Cynthia said. "I just wasn't expecting that." She settled back onto the bed. "I won't make any noise this time, I promise."

I nodded and closed my eyes, breathing in deeply. I formed the image and the emotions again. Krypto started to fidget and whimper in his sleep, his movements getting more frantic as the figure of the bear grew more distinct.

I didn't want Krypto's nightmare to go too long. I could feel his fear and Cynthia's too. I had to make the change quickly.

I changed the feelings of fear and hunger to calm and happiness. Then I had the image of the bear change slowly until it looked like me. Then I had a small inspiration. I formed the bear, much smaller this time, in the palm of my hand and threw it at images of the troublesome raccoons. I hoped Krypto would understand what I was trying to show.

I heard Cynthia take a deep breath. That's when I realized that Krypto wasn't whining any longer. He also wasn't fidgeting in his sleep.

Had I been successful? I wouldn't know until Krypto woke.

I opened my eyes to find Cynthia looking at me with...I don't know. I guess it could have been admiration. It wasn't an expression I was used to seeing directed at me.

"That was amazing, Mik!" she said. "I never should have doubted you."

"I doubted me!" I said, smiling for the first time. "I didn't think I could do it."

"Do you think it worked?"

I shrugged. "I don't know. I guess we'll find out when Krypto wakes up. We should probably go downstairs and let him finish sleeping."

Cynthia nodded. "But before we do that, let's open the window. Phew, but this room smells bad right now."

She walked over to the window and opened it. "Hey, what's this?" she asked, holding up my copy of *The Mystery of Naitaka: Monster or Myth*.

"Oh, that's a book I found here when we first arrived. It's about the local lake monster."

"That's the one that doctor came by your cabin about. Doctor...." Cynthia stopped speaking. "Sorry, I don't remember the name you told me."

"Dr. Gough?" I said. "Yes, that's him. I can't wait to see his camp."

"You're lucky," Cynthia said. "That would be really amazing to see. I mean, what kind of equipment does he have? How will he actually try to find the creature? What will he do if he finds it?"

I had to laugh. Her disbelief switched over to excitement so fast. "Whoa. I don't know any of those answers. At least not yet." We started going down the stairs when I had a thought. "Maybe you can come along."

Cynthia stopped again, halfway down the stairs. "Don't tease me, Mik."

"No, really, Cynthia. Let's go and ask my mom to see what she has to say."

Cynthia shrugged. "I guess. I doubt my mother will ever agree though."

We walked into the living room where Mom and Mrs. Deets were busy chatting.

"Oh, there you two are," Mom said. "I was telling Alice how our family was invited to Dr. Gough's camp. I asked if they might be interested in coming along but I wasn't sure Cynthia would be interested."

"Would you like to go to the scientist's camp? It might be interesting." Mrs. Deets asked, her expression intense. "I know you like science."

"More than anything, Mother!" Cynthia said.

Mom nodded. "Then if Dr. Gough doesn't mind, we will all go to the camp on Saturday."

Cynthia looked stunned and I just stood there wondering if maybe my mother didn't have super powers of her own. Like super-hearing or mind-reading?

That's when I heard the scratching at the door, followed by a single bark. Krypto was downstairs?

Cynthia and I ran to the porch to see Krypto waiting to be let out. I opened the door and he ran out into the yard, eagerly and without hesitation. I could no longer sense the crippling fear he had earlier in the day.

Cynthia and I looked at each other and grinned, sharing a high-five. Sometimes things have a way of working themselves out.

Chapter 23

The next day was Saturday and that meant two things. The first was that my dad was home with Mom and me. I would get two whole days with him! I couldn't wait to tell him all about the raccoons and the grass.

The second thing was that we all got to go to Dr. Gough's camp to see what a real research team did. I could hardly wait. Unfortunately, we weren't going to be picked up for a bit longer so waiting was what I was destined to do.

"So, Mik, what have you got planned for today?" Dad asked me at the breakfast table. He asked the question so innocently that, if I hadn't been able to sense his emotions, I might have been fooled into thinking he'd forgotten about going to Dr. Gough's camp.

I decided to play along. "Gee, Dad, I don't know. I've got to check on the grass and I think Cynthia might be coming over to play." I shrugged my shoulders. "I guess that's about it."

My ploy threw Dad off a little. He did seem confused. Mom too, actually. "Work on the grass and play with Cynthia? That's it?"

I made a show of thinking about his question for several moments. "I guess I could hang out with you too, if you want, Dad."

I obviously did a good job of messing with my dad; something I would have failed at miserably if I hadn't known what he was doing first. He looked at Mom and said, "Milly, is he pulling my leg?"

Mom giggled. "I think you have just had a taste of your own medicine, Harold."

I grinned. "Gotcha, Dad! I know we're going over to Dr. Gough's camp today."

Dad laughed out loud and mussed up my hair. "I guess I had that coming, didn't I, buddy? I've done it to you often enough I should have expected you to pay me back eventually."

"It was the least I could do," I said with a smile.

"So, now that I know you can fool me, tell me about the grass. I hear you've had some interesting adventures with that."

"I suppose. The raccoons came back and were rolling up the sod. It took Mom and me some time to figure that out, but eventually we caught them in the act and fixed the problem."

"That was some good work too," Dad said. "Your mom told me how hard you worked to keep the grass alive. Thank you. Just make sure you get all the nails out when the time comes, please? I would hate to think what they would do going through a lawnmower."

"Yes, sir," I replied. I hadn't really thought of that but I could only guess what might happen.

There was a knock on the door then and Mom and Dad went to answer it. I cast my senses out to feel the emotions of Cynthia, her mother and a man who had to be her father. That was something else I had discovered. People's feelings made them distinct. I could often tell who someone was just by the emotions I felt coming from them. Sort of like a pattern. At least, from people I knew anyway.

I got up from the table and picked up the dirty plates so Mom wouldn't have to. I knew the adults would want to sit and have coffee together, so I did what I could to help out. Mom had already filled the sink with warm, soapy water, so I went to work washing the plates, cups and cutlery while Mom brought our company into the kitchen.

I looked over my shoulder as Cynthia came in. "Hi, Cynthia. I'll be done in just a minute."

"Thank you, Mik," Mom said when she saw what I was doing. "But I could have taken care of those." I sensed her delight at my gesture. It felt good.

"You're welcome, Mom. You were busy and I wanted to help out."

Cynthia came over. "Do you need some help? I could dry the dishes?"

I rinsed of the last plate. "Thanks, Cynthia, but I don't think that's necessary. Mom usually just leaves the plates in the drying rack." I dried my hands on a towel. "See, all done."

"Why don't you and Cynthia go outside and watch for the boat?" Mom suggested.

"But make sure you stay out of the water!" Cynthia's mother said. There was an edge to her emotions as she said it.

"Yes, Mother," Cynthia said. She led me outside. Krypto followed us out of the house.

"Your mother really doesn't like the idea of you being

around water, does she" I asked when we were well away from adult ears.

"No, she doesn't," Cynthia said. "That's one of the reasons I am so glad our mothers like each other. We actually leave the house. If it weren't for coming to see you and your mother, we would stay in the cabin all day every day."

I shook my head. "That doesn't sound very fun." We sat down on a log and looked out at the lake. "I was hoping that having you around would mean we could go canoeing and swimming. I guess that isn't going to happen."

Cynthia sighed. "Not if my mother has anything to say about it."

We sat and watched the lake until we heard the sound of a boat. It wasn't long before the same motorboat that had come by a few days earlier came around a bend in the lake.

"I'll go tell our parents that the boat is here," Cynthia said.

I ran down to the dock to help secure the boat while Cynthia went into the house.

Ω Ω Ω

Cynthia's mother was pretty cautious about her and Cynthia being in the boat. She actually tried to bail on everyone, but her husband convinced her it was all right. Once we were all in, the boat-ride only took ten minutes to get us to the camp.

I was surprised at how close it was to our cabin. It was actually north of the cabin, so further away from Cynthia's cabin than mine.

I'm not exactly sure what I was expecting. Whatever it was, Dr. Gough's camp wasn't it. The first thing I saw was the big green canvas tent huddled about a hundred metres from the lake itself. It looked like one of those army tents you sometimes saw on old war movies.

Around it were several smaller tents. On the lake, there was a long pier that was probably three metres wide with several canoes stacked on top. A grimy yellow, Case backhoe was busy digging a deep hole not far from the water's edge. The hole was partially filled with very black looking water.

Dr. Gough was watching the backhoe work when we came in sight of the camp. He met us on the pier and helped tie the boat up as we were getting out.

Dad was the first to clamber off the boat.

"Welcome to my camp!" Dr. Gough said, shaking my father's hand.

"Thank you for inviting us, Dr. Gough," Dad said. He noticed Mom waiting and reached out to help her off the boat.

Dr. Gough joined him and the two men helped everyone onto the gently swaying pier.

"Please, follow me," Dr. Gough said with a wave. He led the way off the pier and over to the growing hole.

He pointed at the backhoe. "One of my research assistants, Charlie, is the man digging the hole." He yelled a little to be heard over the roar of the machine.

"What is the hole for?" my mother yelled back.

"That will be the holding pond when we capture the creature," Dr. Gough answered. "I have a load of fencing supplies being delivered tomorrow so we can secure the hole." He laughed. "It wouldn't do us much good to capture the beast and have it climb back out and escape, now would it?"

He led us away from the hole and over to the tents. "This is what we like to call our hotelling area. We offer only the finest accommodations for our team." He was grinning when he said it.

I looked into one of the tents as we walked through them.

They were large enough a person could almost stand. The one I saw had a pair of sleeping cots. I got the impression that researchers were a messy lot from that one brief look – cans, a pizza box and a few chip bags littered the floor.

We continued following Dr. Gough through the little tent-town up to the main tent.

"And this is where most of the real research is done." Dr. Gough opened an actual door. "Please come in and I will show you what we are up to."

The tent was large but felt small with all the clutter. A rectangular table, big enough to seat two-dozen people sat in the very middle of the room. A map of what could only be the lake covered almost half the table.

A man and a woman stood at a makeshift camp kitchen, one cooking and the other washing dishes. A wonderful aroma of stew filled the air.

"Let me introduce you to some of my team," Dr. Gough said. "This is Heidi and Max. Heidi is a marine biologist and Max is our sonar expert."

The two smiled and nodded to us as Dr. Gough did the introductions. "Heidi, Max, these are the Murdoch and Deets families. They are neighbours of ours just south of here."

"Good to meet you," Heidi said, with a smile.

"You are all welcome to join us for lunch," Max said. "I've made enough stew for a small army."

"Thank you," Mom said. "We would be glad to have lunch with you all. It smells delicious."

"You're in for a treat," Dr. Gough said. "Max is a wonderful cook."

"But, I thought you said he is your sonar expert," Cynthia's mother said.

Dr. Gough laughed. "When you are a small team like we

are, everyone does whatever is needed. Especially since we work on a shoestring budget. We've got to make our funding last all summer because, once it's gone, we are done and more funding isn't available until at least next year."

"Does that mean Charlie is more than a heavy equipment operator?" Dad asked.

"Heavens yes," Dr. Gough said. "Charlie is actually a paleontologist with a speciality in vertebrates. He also happens to be a former farm-boy who likes to play with heavy equipment."

"And what is your speciality, Dr. Gough," Cynthia's father asked.

I knew the answer to that one. "Dr. Gough has two PhD's: one in Marine biology and the other in evolutionary paleontology."

"That's exactly right, Mik," Dr. Gough said. I could feel and hear his surprise.

I suddenly felt shy and could only mumble, "I did a report on you for school, Dr. Gough. That's how I know."

"I told you he was a fan," Dad said with a laugh.

Everyone joined in the laughter, but I could feel no malice behind it all from anyone. I had to laugh too.

"So, what do you think, Mik?" Dr. Gough asked when the laughter had died down.

"It's all pretty cool, I guess," I said. "It isn't quite what I expected."

"A lot more primitive than you thought it would be, isn't it?"

I had to nod. "Yes. I'm sorry, I don't want to be mean or anything, but—"

"But where are the cool gadgets and trailers to stay in, right?"

Dr. Gough didn't seem *angry*. More expectant, really, but I still couldn't shake the feeling that I had failed a test. "Right," I said, feeling a little miserable.

"I felt the same way the first time I went out into the field to do research," Heidi said from the kitchen area. "I had been expecting everything to be new and clean and perfect." She chortled. "It wasn't. In fact, we barely had an outdoor toilet. It was very eye-opening for me."

I looked at her. "Really?"

"Yup. It was a great experience though. I was still a grad student trying to decide if I wanted to be a field researcher. I had so much fun doing it, I've never wanted to do anything else."

"Wow!" What else was there to say? Heidi's emotions were so strong and positive, I was more sure than ever that I wanted to be part of the expedition too.

"So, are you in?" Dr. Gough asked.

"In?" I wasn't sure at all what Dr. Gough was waiting for, but it was clear from his questions and from his emotions, he expected something.

"Yes. Are you willing to help me with my research this summer?"

I hadn't been expecting that. "Huh?"

"I could really use some more help and your parents said you might be interested. Were they mistaken?"

I looked at Mom and Dad. Mom was carefully keeping her expression, and thoughts, bland. Dad was grinning like he had just heard the best joke ever.

"I...I would love to," I said. My words were followed by a huge surge of disappointment and sadness. I looked to see tears in Cynthia's eyes. It didn't take a genius to figure out she thought I was abandoning her. "But, only if Cynthia can help too!"

"Of course she can help out," Dr. Gough said. "That is, if her parents will allow it."

"What kinds of help did you have in mind?" Mrs. Deets asked. She was guarding her emotions carefully, but something told me she was worried.

"Well, we have some work here around the camp, but I was also hoping Mik and Cynthia might be able to explore some of the waterways that feed the lake, either on canoe or foot."

The carefully guarded emotions were replaced by feelings of horror. Her face reflected the way she felt. "Absolutely NOT! Cynthia is not able to participate in anything to do with the water. She doesn't know how to swim or handle boats of any kind. I won't stand for it." As she spoke, Mrs. Deets voice got louder and louder.

"Mrs. Deets, please don't be alarmed. I wouldn't let the children go out onto the water without proper training. All of my researchers are required to be trained by a certified instructor for both canoe and swimming. In fact, my man Charlie on the backhoe *is* certified for both. He would be providing the training."

"I won't stand for it," Mrs. Deets said again, even more loudly.

"Alice," Mr. Deets said, placing his hand on her arm. "I know how you feel about water and our daughter, but I believe we should consider this."

"Mark, how can you say that?" Mrs. Deets asked, her voice pleading.

"We cannot protect Cynthia from everything for her entire life. She needs to learn how to do things safely. I think this might help her."

"But, Mark—"

"Alice, just a moment." Mr. Deets turned to Dr. Gough. "I'm sorry about this, but there are extenuating circumstances you are not aware of that are causing my wife to panic. I think it would go a long way to ease her mind if the swimming and canoe lessons could be carried out somewhere we could watch."

"How about at our pier?" my dad asked. "The water is deep enough to swim in near the beach and we have a canoe. It isn't too far for anyone to travel and we could all watch them learn."

Dr. Gough shrugged. "I'm sure Charlie wouldn't mind if you don't, Mrs. Deets."

Mrs. Deets took a long shuddering breath and looked at her husband. "I...I don't know about any of this. I guess we could try and see."

That was when I felt Cynthia's emotions again. In the blast of emotions from the adults, I had forgotten her for the moment. Now, she shone through, clear and bright. Feelings of hope with a dose of doubt. But mostly hope.

Chapter 24

We started our lessons the following day. Cynthia and her family came down the pathway about mid-morning and Charlie paddled in on his own canoe shortly after that.

Charlie beached his canoe and climbed out. My father walked to the water to greet him.

I hadn't really seen Charlie when we went to Dr. Gough's camp, so he was a surprise to me. My dad is pretty tall, but Charlie towered over him by several inches. He was also very dark to my father's paler tan.

"Hello, Charlie. I'm Harold Murdoch. I'm really glad you could come by to teach our children how to use a canoe."

Charlie's laugh was rich and deep and when he spoke it was with an accent I hadn't heard before. "It is my pleasure, Mr. Murdoch. Hubert told me your children need to be able to swim and canoe to help with the research. It is my pleasure to teach them."

"Please call me Harold, Charlie," Dad said with a grin. "As you can see, we've all come to watch the show."

"Very well, Harold," Charlie said, shaking Dad's hand. "He looked over at me and Cynthia. Are two you ready to learn how to swim and handle a canoe?"

"You bet," I said. Cynthia nodded, but didn't say anything.

"Excellent! Why don't you put your lifejackets on and we can get started."

Charlie started our lessons then. Mom and Dad entertained the Deets while Cynthia and I got wet. Cynthia came with her lifejacket to wear during the swim lesson. I guess she and her mother weren't willing to risk too much too soon.

That was all right. Cynthia was having fun. So were Krypto and I.

Charlie spent the entire morning teaching us how to float, put our faces in the water and even do a few beginner swimming strokes. I was no expert by the end of the lesson, but I was able to move around in the water better than I had before.

He then switched to teaching us how to use the canoe. He taught us how to get into the little boat first and stay balanced. Then while in the canoe with us, he showed us how to paddle the boat around.

Charlie surprised us when the lesson was over. "Do you two want to take the canoe out?"

Cynthia looked over at her mother who nodded and smiled gently. "As long as you two wear your life jackets, I don't mind."

I was amazed at the change in her attitude. But she did seem a lot more relaxed for some reason. I quietly asked Cynthia while I was pulling on my own lifejacket. "How come your mother is so agreeable?"

"It's cause my father is home," Cynthia said. "Mother is always happier and calmer when he's around."

I wasn't going to complain. Whatever the reason, Cynthia and I were going to be out in the boat by ourselves for the first time ever.

"Now, you two need to be careful," Charlie said. "The lifejackets you are wearing will keep you safe. But if you fool around, you can still get hurt. And I want you to stay reasonably close to shore." He pulled his own lifejacket on. "I'm going to paddle my canoe for a while until you two get the hang of things."

We took the canoe out just like we had learned with Cynthia sitting in the front and me in the back, climbing in after I floated the boat out onto the lake into knee deep water.

Our parents were all seated in lawn chairs watching us. Mom waved and I waved back.

We started to paddle. It was pretty hilarious at first. Cynthia and I were paddling in opposite directions and only managed to spin the boat around in place. Charlie, paddling his canoe around us, was busy splashing water at us and calling out encouragement and directions.

It was a *lot* of fun! Cynthia and I were laughing just about the whole time.

Whenever we got close to shore, Krypto would come swimming out to us.

"I think Krypto wants to ride with us," Cynthia said after he had come out a half dozen times.

"I can pull him into the boat if you don't mind," I said.

"I don't mind. It'll be fun."

So, when Krypto swam out again, I grabbed him and tried to pull him in. The canoe dipped dangerously as I leaned over, threatening to swamp us and Krypto got a little scared.

"Careful, Mik! You're going to sink us," Cynthia said when the boat's edge got too close to the water. She shifted her weight to the other side to try and balance the boat a little better.

I finally managed to get Krypto into the canoe along with a lot of water. I never expected my wet pal to weigh so much. As soon as he was in though, he was standing up in the middle, looking out over the lake, his tail wagging and his tongue hanging out.

"You guys okay out there?" Charlie called from the shore. He had taken his canoe back in almost ten minutes before and had been visiting with the other adults while keeping a close eye on us.

"We're fine, Charlie," I called back. I spent the next several minutes scooping water out of the boat with the bailing can we had in the bottom.

We kept paddling back and forth along the lake, enjoying the day. We had finally gotten the hang of working together and could make the canoe generally go in the direction we wanted. All the while, I noticed a hungry feeling was coming from somewhere. I didn't think it was coming from Cynthia and I knew it wasn't me. Krypto? I focused my attention on him.

I was pretty sure it wasn't him either.

I looked around but didn't see anyone else out on the water. Actually, that wasn't entirely true. There was a motorboat going back and forth near the middle of the lake, but it was currently a long way away. It couldn't be them.

So who?

"What's wrong, Mik?" Cynthia asked. I guess my distraction had been pretty obvious.

"Something or someone is pretty hungry around us. I've been feeling it for a while."

"It's not me," Cynthia said. "I had a good breakfast."

"Oh, I know," I said, rather offhandedly. "I checked you first."

"That's just creepy," Cynthia declared. "Don't you need to ask permission to do that or something?"

I was still searching the lake with my eyes. "Hmm? What?" I looked at my friend. "Sorry. Whatever it is, the feeling is getting stronger. I think it must be getting closer."

"You're impossible!" Cynthia said, her voice angry. Her feelings didn't match her tone though.

Krypto chose that moment to jump out of the canoe back into the lake. The unexpected movement almost tipped us again, forcing Cynthia and me to fight to keep the boat upright.

The hungry feeling vanished and was replaced by something much stronger. More primal. That was when I realized that it wasn't coming from above the water. It was coming from in the water and was getting stronger by the moment!

Krypto was merrily paddling back to the beach, oblivious to the danger I now knew he was in.

"Start splashing the water with your paddle!" I ordered. I slapped my paddle on the water, splashing and making a racket.

"What are you doing?"

"No time to explain, Cynthia. Please, do what I'm doing!" I was watching Krypto closely as I spoke and splashed. He was almost to shore now. Would he make it in time?

The predatory feelings were much closer now. If I were to guess, whatever it was must be almost under the canoe. Cynthia started smacking the water with her paddle.

One of the smacks sounded different from the others. Almost like her paddle struck something much harder than the water.

As it hit, Cynthia said, "I just hit something!"

As she said it, *something* struck the bottom of the boat, raising us slightly out of the water, almost tipping us again. The raw, predatory emotions were instantly replaced by shock and what I can only call a flight instinct.

Then, the emotions were gone.

Krypto stood on the beach, shaking himself off, totally unaware of how close he'd come to being something's lunch.

"What the heck was that?" Cynthia asked, her eyes wide.

"You guys okay out there?" Mom called.

"Fine, Mom," I said waving. I turned my attention back to Cynthia. "Um, you know how you thought it might be cool to see Naitaka on the lake? I think we just came a lot closer than that."

"Wha...you think I hit Naitaka with my paddle?" I could tell the whole idea freaked Cynthia out. Frankly, I was a little freaked out by the whole episode too.

I shrugged. "It all makes sense. Whatever you hit was homing in on Krypto. It was hungry and, as soon as he hit the water, it started hunting him. That's why I wanted you to hit the water with your paddle. I could feel it getting closer and I wanted to scare it away."

"And then I hit it," Cynthia said faintly.

"I think so. It was certainly surprised. I think that's what hit the canoe too."

"I'm ready to go back to shore now," Cynthia said.

"Don't worry. It's gone now."

"I don't care, Mik. I want to go back to shore."

"Okay," I replied. I could feel the panic growing in Cynthia's mind and I didn't want to scare her any further. "Let's go."

We turned the boat and steadily paddled our way back to the shore.

Chapter 25

That little incident almost ended our lessons. Cynthia was understandably freaked out by the whole experience. To be perfectly honest, so was I.

She put on a brave face around the adults, but, when we were alone in my room, she let her guard down.

"Mik, I don't think I want to do anymore swimming or boating lessons. What if that thing comes back?"

I nodded. "I've been thinking about that too, Cynthia. There are lots of people in and around the lake every day. If the creature was attacking people, I'm pretty sure we would have heard about it. Krypto is a lot smaller than us. Maybe that's why it came in."

"I suppose," she said, but I knew she wasn't convinced.

"You know I'll sense it if it comes near us. And we will always have an adult around. Charlie said he would give us more lessons until we're comfortable in and on the water."

"I'm still not sure, Mik," Cynthia said. I could tell she wanted to keep learning to swim and canoe but was worried about the unknown creature.

"Cynthia, I won't let anything sneak up on us. We both know I can sense it coming now. There is lots of summer vacation left. Do you want to spend the whole summer stuck in the house or standing watching the lake?"

"Well…no. But, I don't want to get eaten either."

I couldn't argue with her there. I know I didn't want to be something's lunch. "Just keep telling yourself that we haven't heard of any people being attacked." I ran the whole encounter through my mind. There had been something there. Something smart; it wasn't just animal hunger I had sensed. "I think it might be smart enough to know eating people is a bad idea."

Cynthia looked skeptical. "Are you sure about that or are you just making it up to make me feel better?"

I shrugged. "That's the impression I got. I don't know much for sure."

Cynthia squared her shoulders and gave me a brave smile. "Very well. I'll try to keep swimming and canoeing, but only if you promise to keep watch both with your eyes and your brain."

"Oh, don't you worry about that," I said. "I will definitely be keeping all my senses going at full power."

I saw my book about Naitaka. "You realize you might be the first person to ever smack Naitaka with a paddle, don't you?"

Cynthia smiled. "Yeah. And to think I said how cool it would be to see it swimming around the lake. I guess I should be careful what I wish for."

I laughed. "Yes you should. But if that *was* Naitaka, think of how amazing that is. We were close to a creature most people think is just a myth!"

"It can stay a myth, as far as I'm concerned," Cynthia said. She sounded more like her old self as she spoke.

I knew she would be all right.

Ω Ω Ω

Cynthia and I got another swimming and boating lesson the next day. Cynthia was a little cautious for the first few minutes, but when nothing happened, she started to relax and have fun in and on the water. Just like the day before, Charlie did the teaching while our parents sat on the beach watching and visiting. Dad even brought the cabin's rowboat out on the water. He and Charlie took turns trying to splash us. We all had a game of sponge tag to finish the lesson off.

I couldn't think of a better way to spend the day.

Both our dads went back to work the following Monday, and we kept learning more about swimming and canoeing from Charlie under the watchful eyes of our mothers. We were learning a lot and having fun doing it.

When Cynthia's father went back to work, her mother's calm demeanour started to fade. She was getting more anxious every time we went into the water. When that happened, I...well, I projected feelings of calm and relaxation to her to help her feel better. I suppose you could call it manipulation and it was, of a sort. But I was really trying to see if I could make her feel better.

It worked too. And with every time I did it, it worked better. And I managed it while scanning the lake for our underwater creature.

If Cynthia suspected what I was doing she didn't say anything.

So, we kept swimming and boating and our mothers kept enjoying each other's company. It felt like I was doing the right thing and I was getting better control of my powers.

I didn't want a repeat of the episode with the raccoons and Krypto.

And speaking of the raccoons, Cynthia and I did some exploring when we weren't playing at the lake. We managed to find the family of raccoons deeper in the forest. They were living in a big, dead hollow tree. I felt better knowing they were okay. I hadn't wanted to hurt them, after all. Just scare them away.

Yes, the summer was going great. Maybe not as much excitement as I was normally used to or liked, but we were all enjoying ourselves. The grass had come in well enough with no raccoons to bother it that I was able to remove all the nails.

The week went by quickly. All of the swimming and canoeing were a great distraction. Dad was home almost before I realized he had left.

I woke up to find my parents down having breakfast as per usual.

"Morning, Mik," Dad said as I entered the kitchen.

"Dad!" I rushed over to give him a big hug. "I'm glad you're back."

"Me too, Mik. Me too."

"What would you like for breakfast, Mik?" Mom asked.

"Whatever you and Dad are having is fine, Mom," I said.

"You want liver and onions for breakfast?" Mom asked.

I shuddered at the idea. "Oh, yuck! You're not having *that* are you?" Then I felt her teasing mood and I relaxed a little.

"No, Mik, we are having bacon and eggs. Your favorite," Mom said. She came over and gave me a kiss on the forehead.

"That I would like," I said. I let her think she had fooled me. Her mood was too good for me to spoil.

"Bacon and eggs, coming right up," she said as she bustled over to the stove.

I looked at my dad. "What do you want to do today?"

"I have an idea, but you have to wait until the Deets family gets here."

I was about to protest when Mom placed a plate of bacon and eggs in front of me. My rumbling stomach reminded me what was important. So, I shook my head at my father and began to enjoy my breakfast.

I was about half-finished eating when there was a knock at the door. Dad went to answer it while I tried to shovel the rest of my food into my mouth.

"Slow down, Mik! You'll choke if you don't," Mom said.

"But Mom, Cynthia and her family are here," I mumbled around my food.

"They will wait, now slow down!"

I did as she said, although I still ate fast. Cynthia came running into the room. "Are you ready, Mik? Charlie's already here and he brought Dr. Gough with him too."

"Really?" We hadn't seen anything of the doctor since our visit to his camp. I assumed it was because he was busy. I gulped the last of my milk and got up from the table. "I'll be right there. I've just got to wash my plate quickly."

Mom gently took the plate from my hands. "Out you go, Mik. I know the suspense is killing you. Get out there and find out why Dr. Gough came to see you."

"Thanks, Mom," I said, giving her a quick kiss on the cheek. I followed Cynthia out of the house at a run. Sure enough, Dr. Gough was standing over by the pier talking to Mr. and Mrs. Deets and my dad. Mrs. Deets looked worried and Mr. Deets had his arm around her shoulders. Charlie pretended to work on the boat and not look too conspicuous. Emotional tension radiated from the group in tsunami-sized waves.

I put a hand on Cynthia's arm to slow her down and we casually walked over to the adults.

"...just children!" Mrs. Deets said, her voice shrill.

"I assure you, Mrs. Deets ," Dr. Gough said in a soothing voice, "what I am suggesting is not dangerous in the least. The children will have life jackets on, a two-way radio and continuous check-ins from Heidi whenever they are on the lake."

My father cleared his throat and gave Dr. Gough a warning nod. "Hello, Mik. Hello, Cynthia. We were just talking about you."

Dr. Gough turned to face us. "Hello, you two. How are my young researchers doing this fine morning?" The cheerfulness of his voice and expression were *not* matched by his inner turmoil.

"Good morning, Dr. Gough. It is very good to see you again," I said, in my most adult voice. I stuck out my hand to shake his.

Dr. Gough grinned at my display and shook my hand warmly. "So, Mr. Murdoch. Charlie tells me you and Miss Deets have been working very hard to learn to swim and handle a canoe."

"Yes, sir. Although, I think my skill paddling is much greater than my ability to swim for any distance."

Dad laughed. "That's why you wear the life jackets. They help you swim the distance when you need to. Don't worry. With more practice, you will get as good swimming as you are paddling."

"I suppose."

Cynthia nodded her agreement.

"So, Mik, I'm here to determine if you and Cynthia are

ready for some fieldwork. I really need to get the entire team to start looking for Naitaka. Charlie has the holding pond ready and both Max and Heidi have their equipment ready too."

It was amazing to hear Dr. Gough talk about me and Cynthia as part of his team. That thrill lasted only a moment before Cynthia's mother spoke.

"I'm not sure—"

"Dear, we promised to let the children show us what they can do before we make any decisions," Mr. Deets said.

So that was it! Cynthia and I were being tested. Pass and we might help Dr. Gough with his research. Fail and we would be stuck watching from the shore.

Talk about pressure.

I won't deny I was worried, but what I felt was nothing compared to Cynthia. Her emotions were a jumble of fear, worry, hope and despair. She was starting to panic too. It was time to move or we would be sunk before we started.

I grabbed Cynthia's hand. "Come on. Let's get our life jackets on so we can show everyone how good we are." I sent the lightest surge of encouragement and positive vibes I could to her through our clasped hands.

Cynthia straightened, then nodded and smiled at me. "Let's do this."

We pulled our life jackets on and launched the canoe exactly as we had been taught. Charlie stayed on the pier, calling out a series of different manoeuvres to us.

I won't say we were perfect; far from it, but we did manage to do everything he asked: back-paddling, turning the canoe in place, and a number of other things. We were both sweating and smiling by the time we brought the canoe back to shore.

I could still feel the fear in Mrs. Deets. Some bit of

intuition told me if Cynthia asked to help Dr. Gough, she would be refused so I spoke up.

"Mrs. Deets. I hope you can see how much work Cynthia and I have put into learning to handle the canoe. We both understand being out on the water requires skill and care so we have always kept that in mind." I sent a very fine thread of emotion to her – confidence this time – hoping it might help settle her mind.

"The opportunity to work with Dr. Gough is a dream come true for me, but I can't do it without Cynthia." I let that sink in for a couple moments. "Please, Mrs. Deets. Give Cynthia and me a chance."

Mrs. Deets looked hard at me for almost a minute, not saying anything. I could feel the conflict warring inside her mind. She looked at Dr. Gough. "And you promise that you will stay in constant contact with them?"

Dr. Gough nodded, a serious expression on his face. "I promise. And we have the speed boat so we can get to them quickly if anything goes wrong."

Mrs. Deets shook her head. "I don't know."

"Alice, we've talked about this. You know it will be good for Cynthia," Mr. Deets said.

"Cynthia, is this something you want? You don't have to do it if you don't want to," Mrs. Deets said.

Cynthia shook her head. "I really want to do this, Mother."

Mrs Deets sighed. "Very well."

Chapter 26

"How are you doing, Cynthia?" I asked. We were paddling our way to Dr. Gough's camp. It was our first *official* duty as researchers. Charlie and Dr. Gough followed at a discreet distance in the motorboat.

"I'm okay, Mik," Cynthia said. She sat in the front of the canoe paddling with me stroke for stroke. There was a little unease in her mind, but not too bad.

"You're not worried about anything are you?" I asked.

Cynthia stopped paddling and turned to face me. "You're not in my head right now, are you?"

"Not intentionally," I said. "But I *am* getting something from you."

Cynthia sighed. "I guess I am a little worried. What if that creature attacks us?"

"There isn't any record of it ever having attacked anyone.

And I don't think Dr. Gough would put us at risk either," I said.

"Yes, but what if it does?" Cynthia asked.

"I still have my powers," I reminded her. "They were pretty effective getting rid of the raccoons."

"That may be true, but a raccoon and a lake monster are two pretty different things. I don't think the image of a bear will mean much out here." She started paddling again.

I got back into sync, paddling with her. "Well, what do you think would scare off a lake monster? I can't imagine there are any fish in the lake that would do it."

"I don't know. People, maybe?" Cynthia said, not turning to face me.

I thought about that. Maybe that was why there weren't any Naitaka attacks on people recorded. Maybe the creature, if it actually existed, knew better than to get involved with humans.

"You might be right. Maybe in the past the creature was hunted," I said. "I suppose I could try projecting visions of a hunter of some kind."

I felt Cynthia relax a little. "That sounds good, Mik. I just want to be sure you have a plan if it does come around."

"Tell you what, Cynthia. I will come up with an image while we paddle to the camp and show it to you just before we get there. How does that sound?"

Cynthia nodded and we continued to paddle in silence while I tried to come up with the perfect hunter image.

Ω Ω Ω

We battled some wind on the way to the camp and were both ready for a rest by the time we arrived. Charlie and Dr. Gough went slowly past us in the motorboat when we got within sight of the pier. Charlie waved as they motored past, a big grin on his face.

Heidi and Charlie were both waiting on the shore as we paddled the final distance to beach. Cynthia hopped out as we got to the shallows and pulled the canoe in with Charlie's help.

"Hi, guys! Welcome to Camp Gough. Great to have you on the team," Heidi said, with a big smile.

I climbed out of the canoe and picked up the stern to help Charlie carry it out of the water.

"Thank you, Heidi," Cynthia said, a little shyly. "We're glad to be here." She took Heidi's outstretched hand and tentatively shook it.

I grinned. The energy and enthusiasm I was getting from Heidi was almost intoxicating. "Hello again, Heidi. This is pretty exciting for me."

"Yes, didn't you do a report on the professor or something?" Heidi asked, still smiling.

"Yes, I did," I said. "It was about his expedition in Scotland looking for Nessie."

"Ah yes, I remember that well," she said, a faraway look in her eyes. "I was just a grad student then. That was my first real experience in the field."

"So, you've been with Dr. Gough all along?" Cynthia asked.

"Pretty much," Heidi said. "Not as long as Charlie here, maybe, but a long time."

I looked at Charlie. "When did you start working with Dr. Gough?"

"I think our first expedition was trying to discover the origins of frogs," Charlie said. He said it very matter-of-factly, but there was a strong hint of playfulness coming from him.

I shook my head. "I'm sorry. I don't think I ever read about that research expedition."

He laughed. "No, I'm sure you didn't. Hubert and I were five at the time."

Heidi gave him a playful punch to the shoulder.

He jumped away from the woman and pretended to be hurt. "Ow! You are such a brute!"

"And you are such a tease, Charlie. This is their first time with us and you make fun."

Charlie tried to look apologetic and failed. "Sorry guys."

Cynthia smiled and I felt her nervousness fade. "That's okay, Charlie." She spoke to Heidi then. "Mik and I are used to his jokes by now, Heidi. He was always trying to trick us when we were learning to canoe."

"Don't worry, Cynthia. You will have lots of time to get even with him this summer," Heidi said. "I'll even help." She put her arm around my friend and the two began walking toward the big tent, conspiring quietly with each other.

"I think I'm in big trouble, Mik," Charlie said. "I may need you to have my back." He was grinning as he spoke.

"You got it," I said, already feeling an affinity for the man.

"Come on, Mik. Let me show you the holding pond we built." He led me over to where, only a week before, he had been busy digging with a backhoe.

The holding pond was no longer a small hole. It was now about fifty feet across and roughly circular. I couldn't tell how deep it was; it was filled with water. The whole thing was surrounded by a twelve-foot chain link fence.

"Wow, it's big," I said.

"Has to be," Charlie said with a shrug. "If the creature is what we think it is, it is likely at least fifteen feet long.

We need something big enough to hold it and give it some room to move too. And, of course, we've got to keep it from escaping and people from getting at it."

"What happens after you capture the creature?" I asked. "That is, if you capture it?"

"Hubert has made arrangements with a research facility that has a large freshwater tank we can use. The creature will be moved there for study," Charlie said.

"Will it be released after Dr. Gough studies it?" I asked.

"I doubt it," Charlie said. "Something like that is too valuable. Scientists like Hubert will study it while it is alive and probably dissect it after it dies to get even more information."

Charlie went quiet for a few moments and I could feel his emotions churning like he was trying to come to some decision. He must have, because he looked at me with a serious expression I hadn't seen before.

"I probably shouldn't tell you this, but Hubert is trusting you a great deal just by having you work with us." He stopped speaking and watched me until I nodded. "You know the expedition to Loch Ness in Scotland the doctor went on?"

"Yes. He wasn't able to prove the creature existed," I said.

"That isn't entirely true," Charlie said. "We had Nessie cornered in a small lagoon with a net. We think some of the locals came and cut the net to let her escape."

"Why would they do that?" I asked.

"We were never able to prove they did it, but I got the impression Nessie was an important part of the area. They didn't want to lose the creature to scientific discovery. The mystery was worth more than what we could do if we caught it."

The enormity of his admission stunned me. Dr. Gough

had captured Nessie? Really? And the world didn't know? There was only one thing I could say. "Wow."

"I know, right?" said Charlie. "But we have no proof and science is all about facts. To claim we found Nessie without any corroborating facts would put Hubert's credibility at risk."

"I won't say anything," I said.

"Thank you, Mik. I'm telling you this because we all rely on each other. I trusted Hubert's judgement about you and your friend Cynthia when he first mentioned you helping. Now that I've had a chance to work with you with the canoeing, I know he was right."

Charlie's words and feelings about the matter were so serious, I could only nod. I felt a strong sense of protectiveness from him for Dr. Gough too.

That loyalty only made me want to help Dr. Gough that much more.

Charlie showed me around the rest of the camp before taking me up to the main tent where we found Heidi and Cynthia pouring over the large map of the lake.

"Mik, look here. This is where we are," Cynthia said, calling me over to the table. She pointed out the spot on the map where the camp was marked with a large red star.

"So, that would make my cabin be about here," I said, tracing my way back along the outline of the lake to what I thought was the right spot.

"Close," said Heidi. "Actually, your cabin isn't quite that far. That would be where Cynthia lives." She back-tracked a short way toward the camp. "I think this is where you live."

I looked to where she was pointing. Of course, the buildings weren't showing on the map so I really couldn't tell.

"Here's the small river between our cabins," Cynthia said,

showing me the thin blue line representing the water. "And here is the pathway and bridge."

When she pointed those features out, it made more sense to me. "Oh, I see."

Heidi pointed out several of the thin blue lines that were near our cabins. "Dr. Gough was hoping you and Cynthia might be able to check these tributaries out. They aren't really big enough to take the boat down and it would help us to focus on other parts of the lake. Maybe by spreading out we will have better luck finding Naitaka."

I nodded. That made sense. The search team wasn't very big so looking in multiple areas would help. "What are we looking for, exactly?"

"It could be almost anything. You might see strange ripples in the water, or pathways that lead right up to and into the water," Charlie said. "In Scotland, we found flipper imprints in soft soil areas and what had to be marks from a heavy body."

"Would we hear anything?" I asked. "Cynthia and I heard something a week or so ago when we were out for a walk. Krypto got really excited too."

Charlie considered that. "Were you near the water anywhere?"

"I think so. The bush was too thick for us to be sure, but when we followed the tree line, it brought us to the river," I said.

"Anything is possible," Charlie said. "Mind you, it could have been some sort of waterfowl too."

"I suppose," I said, not quite believing Charlie's possible explanation.

"Here is a camera to take pictures of anything you see," Heidi said, pulling out a small digital camera. "Bring back the camera every few days so we can download the pictures for review and change the batteries. And, it's not waterproof, so maybe keep it in a freezer bag when you are travelling so it stays dry until you need it."

Cynthia took the camera from Heidi. "We will take good care of it."

Heidi smiled. "You also need this two-way radio. It is waterproof, has a built-in GPS and floats. If you get into any trouble, call in immediately. Any one of us will hear you. To use the GPS, press this button and it will give you the coordinates." She handed to radio to Cynthia and quickly showed her how to use the GPS function. "Here are also a couple smaller maps of the area immediately around your cabins."

"What kind of trouble," Cynthia asked, looking a little worried as she took the radio and maps from Heidi.

"Anything really," Heidi said. "Your canoe might tip over and you could need some help getting it turned back over and emptied of water."

"Or maybe the creature could attack us?" Cynthia asked.

Charlie laughed. "Probably not, Cynthia. It hasn't ever happened before, so I wouldn't worry too much."

Charlie looked at his watch. "I've got to get out on the water searching and you two need to get home so your folks don't worry. Tomorrow should be soon enough to start searching." He led us out of the tent.

"Okay, Charlie," I said.

He and Heidi escorted us back down to the canoe.

"One last thing," Heidi said. "I want you two to radio in regularly when you are searching. Check in when you start and every hour with your location, okay? We don't want to lose either of you."

"Is it okay if we take Krypto with us?" I asked.

"Krypto?" Heidi asked.

"That's Mik's dog," Charlie said. "Sure, I don't see any reason why you couldn't. And make sure you have bottles of water and some food whenever you go out. Believe it or not, paddling out on the lake can dehydrate you quickly."

Cynthia and I got into the canoe and Charlie gave us a starting push to get going on the water.

Heidi waved as we back-paddled into deeper water. "Have fun you two and remember to call in, okay? I'll see you both in a few days."

We waved at Heidi and got underway for home. I was still a bit tired and was grateful the wind was at our back.

Chapter 27

The next day Cynthia and I paddled toward the small river we had both walked across dozens of times. We hadn't discussed it at all; I think we both knew instinctively we needed to search it first. Krypto lay comfortably in the middle of the canoe guarding our lunch and watching the world go by. We called in to Heidi to let her know where we were exploring before we entered the creek.

I felt a thrill as we passed under the bridge. We might be about to solve not only the mystery of the strange splashing sounds from several days before, but we might even find Naitaka!

I knew Cynthia felt it too.

Within half a dozen strokes of the paddle, we were past the bridge. Trees hugged the shoreline like a thick wall, sometimes hanging right over the water. The waterway wasn't more than twenty feet across and the only sky we could see was a thin ribbon almost crowded out by greenery.

It felt a lot like the first time I had been in a church. Quiet, serene and filled with mystery.

"Mik, you don't feel the creature nearby, do you?" Cynthia asked before we were very far down the river. Her voice and emotions were both nervous.

"Nope. Nothing so far," I said. I hadn't actually been trying to feel for the creature, being too caught up in the new experience of the watery cathedral. I cast my senses out as I spoke, feeling just a little guilty at my fib.

Nothing. Other than the nervous feelings from Cynthia and the drowsy dreams of my pup, everything seemed quite ordinary.

We continued to paddle for the better part of thirty minutes before the radio crackled with Heidi's voice. "Mik? Cynthia? How are you two doing?"

Cynthia stopped paddling and picked up the radio. "Hello, Heidi. We're fine, thanks. How are you?"

"I just thought I would check in with you two. Make sure everything is all right. Where are you at?"

"We've been in that waterway between our cabins for about thirty minutes or so, Heidi. Hang on a second." Cynthia pressed a button on the side of the radio and took a GPS reading. "According to the GPS on the radio, our coordinates are 53°03'54.5" North, 114°09'51.4" West if that helps."

"Cool. Hold on a minute. Did you say 51.4 seconds west?"

"Yes."

"Okay, I know where you are now. I'll check back with you in an hour or so. And, just so you know what to expect, the creek you're on right now is fed by underground sources. You will probably come to a pond or dead end at some point where the water goes underground."

"Okay, Heidi. Thank you," Cynthia said.

"Remember to take pictures and, if you find anything, radio in right away, okay?"

"You got it, Heidi. Bye for now," Cynthia said. She put down the radio, stowing it under her seat and picking up the paddle. It only took her a few strokes before we were paddling in sync once again.

"Do you think we will find anything, Mik?" Cynthia asked without looking back.

"I don't know. I hope so," I said. "Wouldn't it be awesome if we actually found Naitaka?"

"I'd rather we didn't," Cynthia said. "The whole idea scares me."

It wasn't until she said the words I realized how big a sacrifice Cynthia was making for me. She must have been holding it very tightly in her mind because I hadn't an inkling of it until I knew what to look for.

"Thank you for doing this. I know you agreed to come along so I could explore," I said.

Cynthia stopped paddling and carefully turned to face me. "I know how important it is to you to help Dr. Gough. I didn't want to get in the way of that. Besides," she smiled then, "I can't let you have *all* the fun."

"Well, thank you just the same," I said, as we regained our paddling synchronisation. I cast my senses out again. Other than the three of us in the canoe, and what I guessed might be a squirrel somewhere off in the trees, I sensed nothing unexpected.

We canoed for another thirty minutes, our paddles dipping into the water in steady strokes. I was grateful the river didn't flow any faster or it would have been hard work. As it was, we were able to make good headway without too much effort.

The river started to widen then and we were able to see

more of the sky. A few minutes more paddling and it opened right up into a good-sized pond.

To the left of where we came into the pond were pussy willows and a mass of bullrushes and cattails too thick to paddle through. A red-winged blackbird clung to one of the cattails, trilling before leaping into the air and flying deeper into the marsh.

Trees surrounded the rest of the pond in a continuous wall and, on the far right side, a patch of sand ran out of the water.

"What do you think, Mik? Can we beach our canoe on the sand and have a snack?" Cynthia asked.

"Sounds good to me," I said. I rotated my shoulders to take the kinks out. "I could use a break from paddling too. We've been at this for over an hour."

I turned the canoe toward the beach and we paddled hard to force the canoe up onto the sand. I tried to probe for the bottom of the pond with my paddle and wasn't able to hit anything solid.

"Careful when you get out, Cynthia. This pond feels really deep."

"Okay, Mik. Sit tight and I'll pull the canoe up on the beach so you can get out too."

Cynthia clambered over the bow of the canoe and stepped out onto the sand. Her feet sunk almost and inch into the soft sand before she gained a foothold. "Wow, this ground is really soft. Take care getting out, Mik." She pulled the canoe more than halfway onto the sand and held it steady for me.

Krypto got to his feet and jumped out, and I grabbed our basket of food as I climbed out. I carried the basket further out onto the sand and set it down. Cynthia and I then pulled the canoe the rest of the way out of the water.

The sun was shining full onto this part of the beach and

the sand was wonderfully warm. It was littered with bird tracks and leaves along most of the surface except one area that looked like it might have been swept smooth. I pulled off my life jacket and shoes and sat down, enjoying being out of our boat. Cynthia grabbed the radio out from under the seat of the canoe and sat down beside me.

She pressed the talk button on the radio. "This is Cynthia calling Heidi. Hello, Heidi?"

We waited for a few moments before Heidi's voice crackled through the radio's speaker. "This is Heidi. Is everything all right, Cynthia?"

"Everything is fine, Heidi. We found the end of the river. It's a big pond like you said. Mik and I are stopping for a rest and then we're going to head back."

"Is there anything interesting there?" Heidi asked.

"A really nice beach on one side of the pond, but really not much else," Cynthia said. "I'll take a few pictures so you can see what it looks like."

"Thank you, Cynthia. Talk to you in an hour. Heidi out."

Cynthia set the radio down in the sand beside her and lay back. "This is really peaceful. I could lie here all day."

I was about to agree with her when Krypto started barking. I looked over to where he was busy digging at a mound of sand.

Now what?

I sighed and climbed to my feet to see what had him so excited. Cynthia was up moments later.

Krypto stopped digging as we approached and gave me a, *look what I found* sort of bark. He used his nose to move a bit more sand.

I dropped to my knees and began pulling sand away from the mound. "What have you found, Krypto? What's got you so excited?" That's when my fingers scraped something hard and smooth.

It was warm.

I carefully brushed more of the dry sand away from the object.

I leaned closer to look at it, not quite sure I could believe what I was seeing.

"What have you found, Mik?"

I jumped. I had momentarily forgotten Cynthia was there. What was under my fingertips was too incredible. I looked dumbly up at my friend.

"Wha?" I said in my most intelligent manner.

Cynthia knelt on the sand beside me. "Mik? What have you found?"

I moved aside to give her a better look. I gently moved Krypto out of the way too.

"Mik, is that what I think it is?"

I brushed more sand away from the object. I nodded. "Yes, it's an egg."

Chapter 28

The egg was big. I don't mean chicken egg big. I mean big like a football big. It was white with mottled patches of yellow and brown and was warm to the touch.

"What should we do with it, Mik?" Cynthia asked, looking carefully at it. "What do you think it's from?"

I shook my head. "It's way too big to be from a turtle. If I were to guess, I would say we just stumbled across an egg from Naitaka. What we should do is take a picture of it and call into the camp to tell them what we found."

"I'll get the camera," Cynthia said. She jumped to her feet and collected the camera from her backpack. She turned it on and started to take pictures.

"What do you think Dr. Gough will do with it?" Cynthia asked as she took the pictures.

I shrugged. "Study it, I suppose."

"Do you think it will hatch?"

That got me thinking. Would the egg hatch? Would Dr. Gough try to hatch it and raise the creature that came from it? Would the egg even survive?

"I don't really know. I mean, moving the egg might kill it. Maybe we should cover it back up and leave it here. We can still call in and the team can come here to see it. They might just leave it to hatch naturally," I said. Even as I spoke I knew leaving the egg where it sat was unlikely at best. Dr. Gough had lost Nessie in Scotland because he had left it alone. I didn't think he would make that mistake again.

"So, we should call it in," Cynthia said.

"I guess," I replied. It didn't feel quite like the right thing to do, but it was what we had agreed.

"Okay." Cynthia fetched the radio and sat down beside me. "You found the egg. Do you want to call?"

I smiled. "Thanks, Cynthia, but technically, Krypto found the egg."

"Yeah, but Krypto can't talk or operate the radio. And he is your dog."

"I can't argue with you there," I said, taking the radio from Cynthia.

I depressed the talk button. "Mik calling Heidi. Are you there, Heidi?"

Heidi answered almost immediately. "Mik? Why are you calling in so soon? Is everything all right?"

"Everything is fine, Heidi." I was about to tell her about the egg when Krypto starting to bark. It wasn't his normal, *hey, look at me*, bark either. It was more of a, *something is very VERY wrong and I need you to pay attention* barks.

"Hold on, Heidi. Krypto's excited about something." That's when I noticed the expression on Cynthia's face. It was a cross between scared and terrified. Her feelings slammed at me like a hammer at almost the same time.

"Mi...Mik!" Cynthia's voice was a terrified whisper. Her eyes never left a point somewhere over my head and told me I really needed to turn around immediately and carefully. Krypto continued his furious barking somewhere behind me.

I turned and looked up. My brain had some trouble registering what I was seeing. My eyes followed the long, sinuous grey neck that rose out of the water up, up, up. A vaguely horselike head with large intelligent eyes glared down at Cynthia and me.

I scrambled back away from the creature in a desperate crab-walk. Cynthia followed me across the beach. We moved as far toward the trees as we could, watching the creature the entire way.

I could feel it now. Its emotions weren't as terrifying as its appearance, but the creature was both worried and protective. Those feeling were directed at the large egg we had found.

"Wha...what are we going to do?" Cynthia whispered to me. She was shaking and was trying desperately not to panic.

"I don't know." I turned my attention to Krypto who continued to bark, rushing the water and jumping up and down.

The creature began to lean toward the egg, never taking its eyes off of Cynthia and me. Krypto leapt to try and grab the thing, but it was too quick. It nudged at Krypto with its head, knocking him rolling across the sand.

I couldn't let my pal remain in danger. I jumped to my feet and bolted over to him. My mind was whirling. What could I do to protect Cynthia, Krypto and me?

I grabbed Krypto and held onto him, stopping him from

charging the creature again. Krypto's emotions were jumbled. He was worried about me and, at the same time, eager to play with the big creature.

"Settle down, boy," I said as I held him tight. The creature had taken it pretty easy on my dog the first round, but there was no telling what it would do if Krypto bounded at it again.

I sent soothing thoughts at Krypto. I had to get my dog under control or risk losing him to the monster. In my excitement, I didn't even try to keep my powers under control and only affect Krypto. I broadcast them, hitting everything with a brain in the vicinity.

I didn't even realize I was doing it until I noticed that the creature's emotions had shifted from worried and hostile to more curious.

It leaned toward its egg and nosed at it, rocking it gently. Apparently satisfied that the egg was all right, Naitaka, for it surely was Naitaka, re-covered the egg with the warm dry sand. I could feel its affection and love for the egg as it cared for it.

When it was done, Naitaka turned its attention back to Cynthia, Krypto and me. It regarded us, almost as if deciding what to do with we intruders.

I adjusted my emotional projections to feelings of friendship.

Even as I did that, I felt a pang of guilt flash through my mind. How could I possibly mislead this magnificent creature if I were planning to reveal it to Dr. Gough? At the same time, how could I not tell Dr. Gough about its existence?

What was I going to do?

"Mik?" Heidi's voice crackled from the radio I still held in my hand.

I jumped a little. I had totally forgotten I had called Heidi.

I pressed the talk button making sure to maintain my hold on a squirming Krypto. "Heidi?"

"Mik, what's going on there? Are you all right? Why was your dog barking like that?"

I had to think quickly. I still didn't know whether to tell the team about the egg or Naitaka yet. My mind said one thing and my heart another.

"Everything is okay here, Heidi. Sorry, false alarm. Let me call you back at our normal check-in time." My eyes never left Naitaka as I spoke. The creature continued to watch me with what I could only guess was curiosity. At least, that's what I garnered from its emotional state.

Heidi's next words sounded skeptical. "Are you sure, Mik?"

"Oh yeah. We're fine. Krypto just saw a family of squirrels."

"Whatever you say, Mik. Talk to you in an hour. Heidi out."

"Mik, why didn't you tell Heidi about the creature?" Cynthia said, her voice quiet. "Don't you think we could use the help?" That last sentence was accompanied with a flash of fear and uncertainty from Cynthia.

I kept watching Naitaka as I replied to Cynthia. "I don't know why I didn't tell her. This creature isn't trying to harm us so why would I tell them?"

"Because you said you would report anything you find?" Cynthia said. "Aren't we working with Dr. Gough's team to find and capture this thing?"

"Yes," I said with a nod. "But, do you know what they are going to do to Naitaka if they capture it? They are going to move it out of the lake and study it."

"So?"

"They won't ever return it." I looked away from Naitaka then and caught Cynthia's eye. "Naitaka will be stuck in an aquarium somewhere and studied for the rest of its life and beyond. It didn't seem to matter before, but this creature is going to be a mother. It doesn't seem right to let it be caught now."

Krypto let out a low growl and I felt something nuzzle my hair from behind. I increased my grip on my dog and turned my head to come nose-to-nose with Naitaka. The creature had nibbled gently at my hair. It's thoughts continued to be curious and, I thought I could feel the faintest undertone of friendliness.

I took a surprised step back and Naitaka jerked its head up and away from me. I made my way to Cynthia and handed her the radio.

"If you want to make the call to Heidi to report Naitaka, go ahead," I said. "I won't stop you. But I think we need to keep this secret. I don't know why, but it seems like the right thing to do."

Cynthia sighed. "I don't know what the right thing is, Mik. But the creature doesn't seem to be a threat right now. I suppose we can hold off making a decision for the moment."

"Maybe we should head back and think about it some more," I said.

"Do you think it will let us leave?" Cynthia asked.

"There's only one way to find out," I said. "I can go out into the canoe and see if it will let me. If it does I can come back for you."

"No," Cynthia said, quite firmly. "We will go together. I don't want you to leave me alone on this beach."

"Have it your way. I wouldn't abandon you. I just thought, if I got into trouble on the water, you could call for help."

"No. We will go together. That's the end of it."

There was no point arguing with Cynthia. I could tell she wasn't about to change her mind.

The creature was still in the water watching us when we came to our decision.

"Naitaka," I said, addressing the creature. "We are going to leave here. I promise, we won't tell anyone about your egg, okay?" I continued to project feelings of peace and friendship at the creature as I spoke.

It cocked its head at me and moved back from the beach a short way.

I took that as a good sign and moved toward the canoe. When the creature made no attempt to stop me, Cynthia followed bringing our gear.

I hadn't put Krypto down yet. He was still squirming in my arms, but I couldn't be certain what he would do. I placed him into the canoe and pushed it halfway into the water.

"You coming, Cynthia?" I asked. "If you wouldn't mind holding the canoe while I climb in and then push off?"

"Okay, Mik." Now that we were doing something, Cynthia seemed more confident.

I climbed into the canoe and manoeuvred around Krypto to take my spot in the stern. It was a little unnerving having my back to the creature, but I could still sense its emotions; it remained curious rather than angry. The hairs on the back of my neck stood up as I tried to act cool and calm, all the while projecting feelings of peace and friendship as Cynthia placed our gear into the canoe and pushed off the shore and scrambling in.

I backpaddled and we managed to slide off the beach. We turned the canoe just as Naitaka slipped under the water. I felt it move swiftly away from us, but not down the river. It seemed to swim beyond the edge of the pond and under the ground, eventually disappearing from my mind.

It didn't make any sense at all.

"Mik, come on!" Cynthia said, pulling me out of my

reverie. "We've got to get back home. Maybe we can figure out what to do next."

"Sure thing, Cynthia," I said. I began to paddle, working to match Cynthia stroke for stroke. I tried to focus on the canoe and water, but I couldn't rid myself of the image of the egg and Naitaka looming over us at the beach. It could have attacked us. It would have been right to do so to protect its unhatched young. But it hadn't. It had been curious about us.

That might have been due to my powers, but what if it wasn't a dangerous creature? I *had* sensed feelings from it, after all. Sure, some of those were predatory, but it had to eat just like everything else. It had also seemed to listen to us when we spoke to it. It had seemed to understand us. Did that mean it could think like we do. *And* it had gently covered the egg in warm sand just like my mom tucked me in at night.

Just like my mom.

Would we be right in turning it over to Dr. Gough?

Chapter 29

Neither of us spoke the entire way back to the cabin. We didn't even speak when we pulled the canoe out of the water to tip it over on the canoe rack near the pier.

I was starting to wonder if either of us would ever talk again. I didn't know what to say. I didn't have any answers. From the whirlwind of emotions that swirled around Cynthia, I wasn't sure she knew what to say or do either.

Cynthia picked up her backpack and started to walk toward the path.

I had to stop her. I needed her to help me work my way out of the problem. I knew I couldn't do it myself. "Cynthia, please stop!"

She stopped walking, standing very straight and very still, facing away from me.

"Cynthia, I need your help. I don't know what to do."

She shook her head, still facing away from me. "What

makes you think I have any idea, Mik?" She turned then and I could see the beginning of tears in her eyes. The swirling emotions had stopped and were replaced by fear. Nothing but fear.

"Mik, I was scared to death back there. It was all I could do to not scream. You ask me what I think we should do? I think we should tell Heidi or Charlie or Dr. Gough about the creature. Maybe if they capture it I won't feel so scared every time I look at the water."

I nodded. "I was scared too. But I didn't sense any malice coming from Naitaka. It was curious about us more than anything."

"And what happens if it decides we are the enemy? What then?"

"I don't know, Cynthia. I was using my powers when it showed up. I used them to calm Krypto and I directed them at the creature. Maybe I have it under my control?" I didn't believe it for a minute. I don't think Cynthia did either.

"And if you didn't? I don't know, Mik. Right now, I don't want to do this anymore."

"Tell you what, Cynthia. Let's not make any decisions right now. Sleep on it and we can talk some more tomorrow, okay?"

"Sure, Mik, but I don't know that sleep will change anything."

"I don't know that it will either, but it can't hurt. Now, how about I walk you home? Let me tell Mom where we are going and then Krypto and I will come with you."

Cynthia smiled. "Thanks, Mik. I would like that. I'm still pretty freaked out."

"Stay here," I said. "I'll be right back to walk you home."

ΩΩΩ

That night I climbed into bed still thinking about the creature. It was amazing enough that Cynthia and I, two kids, found it in the first place. Even with my powers it seemed so unlikely. But to have actually been up close?

I shook my head and pulled the covers up a little tighter to my chin.

Amazing.

I closed my eyes, trying to get to sleep, but my brain whizzed and whirled with questions and ideas. Naitaka had acted curious. It had treated its egg gently and with care. It hadn't attacked Cynthia and me the way so many protective mothers in the wild would.

Should we tell Dr. Gough about it?

Stories and legends surrounded the creature from hundreds of years before. Was the creature that old or just one of many generations of the same beast? If that were true, were there others in the lake? What would capturing this one do to it?

Should we tell Dr. Gough about it?

It hadn't attacked us or even tried to frighten us. In fact, it had nuzzled my hair just like a horse had done once before at my Uncle Greg's farm. It had acted friendly toward us. Was that simply my power affecting it or was it truly that peaceful?

Should we tell Dr. Gough about it?

That question kept coming around in my thoughts. Did Cynthia and I even have the right to take away something that was part of the local legends? At the same time, did we have the right to keep it secret from Dr. Gough and team when we had both solemnly promised to help out in the search?

Somewhere in there I must have drifted off. That didn't keep the questions from hitting me though. It was late at night when I woke up with an urgent need to use the bathroom.

I climbed out of bed, careful not to dislodge Krypto who slept on top of my covers at my feet. I tiptoed to the bathroom, trying my best to remain quiet. I could hear the soft breathing and occasional snore that came from my mother's bedroom.

I opened the bathroom door and stepped in, not turning on the light. I closed the door behind and reached for the light switch.

My fingers brushed against the wall and I felt soft cool moss instead of the flat painted surface I had expected.

I gasped and tried to find the light switch but my hands and fingers only rubbed up against the irregular spongy surface. I felt around, but couldn't find the doorknob any more either.

I was starting to panic. My heart was beating faster and faster.

That is when the room started to brighten, not from an overhead light, but from glowing moss all around me. It got brighter and brighter until I could see that I was not in my bathroom like I thought, but in a different place entirely. One I hadn't ever expected to see again.

The Cave of Wonders.

I know I should have considered how I had gotten there, but my mind was oddly at peace once I recognized the location. I stood where I was and looked across the still waters of the Cave's lake toward the orchard. The same orchard that had given my friend, Miss Purdy, her super powers. In fact, the very same orchard that had produced the berry that gave me my own ability to feel other's emotions.

I felt eyes on me and turned to look at where the cavern walls rounded and the path wound around the lake.

A wolf sat on its haunches, watching me. That didn't cause me any alarm either because I recognized this wolf. It was the animal form of the Guardian of the Cave.

No sooner did I recognize the wolf than it transformed into the familiar human form of the Guardian. He strode toward me, a grim expression on his face.

I tried to greet him, but my throat was frozen. My feet refused to move and I was like a statue standing by the water as he came toward me.

"You must not tell the doctor of Naitaka," the Guardian said to me. "It is a sacred creature. One of the last of its kind. It is your duty to protect it and others like it. Do you understand?"

I was able to nod my understanding. My tongue and mouth still refused to respond.

"You have questions for me?"

My tongue and mouth began to work then. "Why is Naitaka so important? Isn't it wrong for me to break my promise to Dr. Gough? What can I do?"

The Guardian's severe expression thawed a little. "Mik, Naitaka and its ancestors have been part of this land since before history. The first people to come here found the creature already living and guarding the lake. It is a part of the very spirit of the land." The Guardian knelt in front of me, placing his right hand on my shoulder. "It is laudable that you would want to keep your promise to your Dr. Gough. Being truthful and trustworthy are noble virtues for any hero. However, I cannot tell you what to do about your promise. Search your heart and perhaps you will come up with a suitable compromise."

I couldn't imagine what a suitable compromise could be. I mean, I either kept my promise and told Dr. Gough or I didn't. Still, I knew in my heart that allowing Naitaka to be captured was wrong.

"I will do my best to keep Naitaka safe, Sir."

"Very good. When you wake, you will find you are holding a stone. Your friend Cynthia will know your story is truth when you show it to her. Do you understand?"

Once again, I nodded.

"That is well, Mik Murdoch. Now, return to your own place and speak of this to no one but Cynthia. And remember to protect Naitaka and its kind."

Ω Ω Ω

"Cynthia, you will never guess what happened to me last night!"

Cynthia, who had only just cleared the trees to see me running at her like a crazy man, took a step back. Her mother, who was a few steps behind her on the path, laughed and walked past us, shaking her head at my antics.

I waited until she was out of hearing before I spoke again. "Cynthia, the most amazing thing happened." I held out the stone the Guardian had given me. "And it involves this stone."

Cynthia's eyes widened when she saw the stone. She came closer to get a better look at it, digging in her pants as she moved.

"But, it was only a dream," she said. "Wasn't it?" Cynthia held out an identical stone to me.

So, that's what the Guardian meant when he said she would know my story to be true. I felt my hopes rise. Maybe Cynthia had the answer I needed.

"What happened in your dream?" I asked.

Cynthia's brow furrowed for a moment before she answered me. "I was in a huge cave. It wasn't dark at all because the walls glowed. There was a small lake in the middle of it."

"That was the Cave of Wonders you saw. I've been there, once before," I said.

"That's what the man said."

"The man?" I asked.

"Yes. A man appeared and told me he knew you. He said you would need my help to make a difficult decision."

"Did he say what my decision should be," I asked, hoping he had given Cynthia the answer denied to me.

She shook her head. "No. Just that you had to decide what to do about Naitaka and that it was something I could help you with."

I sighed. "Is that all?

Cynthia nodded. "In my dream he gave me this stone. When I woke up, it was sitting on my night stand. I brought it because I thought you might know what it was."

"I do," I said. "It is proof. Proof that we need to figure out what to do about Naitaka."

"What if we just pretended that we hadn't found anything?" Cynthia asked.

I considered the suggestion. "You mean, never telling Dr. Gough what we found or just waiting?

She shrugged. "Either. Maybe we give the egg a chance to hatch and then we tell him."

"Maybe," I said. "The egg shell might be enough to satisfy him, but it might also convince him to keep looking." I thought a little longer. "You know, I think we should tell him...eventually. I don't want to be dishonest with Dr. Gough and we did make a promise."

"Yes we did," Cynthia agreed. "But when...." She looked like she was thinking hard

"What is it?"

"We took pictures of the egg, Mik. How are we going to explain that when we turn in the camera's memory card in a few days?"

"I don't know." I thought for a second. "Do you have the camera?"

"Yes." Cynthia pulled the camera out of her bag and handed it to me.

I carefully turned the camera around, looking for someplace to plug it into a computer. On the bottom right corner was a cover to what I could only assume was a battery compartment. I opened the compartment and had to juggle for a moment to catch the two AA-batteries that immediately fell out.

"Careful, Mik!"

I smiled and handed Cynthia the compartment panel and two batteries. "Hold these for me for a minute, please?"

I looked inside the camera. There was the mini-memory card to hold the digital pictures. And right below it was a small cable port. I held it up for Cynthia to see. "Look here. A port to plug a cable in. I bet if Mom has the right cable, I can plug this camera into her computer and delete the pictures of the egg off the camera."

"Do you think you should? I mean, it isn't our camera."

"It's either that or give Dr. Gough the pictures of the egg. Besides, this camera is a lot like my mom's camera. I've used it hundreds of times."

"Okay, Mik. If you say so."

"That reminds me," I said. "You didn't take any pictures of Naitaka too, did you?"

Cynthia shook her head. "I didn't think of it until it was gone. I was too scared."

"That's good. Come on. Let's go into the house and check for the right cable."

Chapter 30

We went right up to Mom's room where she kept her laptop and looked through her computer bag. There were cables, but nothing that would work for the camera.

I slumped down on the bed. "I guess that idea is shot. Now what are we going to do?"

Cynthia was looking from the camera to the laptop. "Mik, isn't this a memory card slot on your mom's laptop?"

"Yeah, so?" I said. "We can't plug the camera into a memory card slot."

"Maybe not, but we can plug the camera card into it," Cynthia said. She delicately reached into the camera's battery compartment and with a gentle tug, pulled the camera's memory card out. She held it up for me to see. "Now we should be able to plug the card into the laptop and delete the files, right?"

I jumped off the bed. "Of course! You are brilliant." I took the offered memory card and plugged it into the laptop's card slot. I opened the software's file window and held my breath.

For several moments, nothing happened. Then, with a chirpy bing, an icon showed up in the window representing the memory card.

I let my breath out, hearing it echo out from Cynthia. I double-clicked on the icon and a list of files showed up. I clicked on a file icon so the files showed up as small thumbnail-sized icons that were miniature versions of the pictures.

We quickly deleted every file that had a picture of the egg. That done, I replaced the card and batteries in the camera. It wasn't until the battery compartment door snapped back on that I could breathe a sigh of relief.

"Now what are we going to do?" Cynthia asked. "Sure we've removed the pictures of the egg, but Dr. Gough and the team could still find and capture Naitaka."

"I wish we could just hide Naitaka so they couldn't find her."

"We could search online for something like that."

I thought about that. It wasn't as crazy an idea as it sounded although I doubted we could search for *Naitaka hiding places* and expect to get anywhere.

"We could. Let me ask Mom if we can use the Internet for a few minutes, okay? You think of search phrases while I'm gone."

"Okay, Mik."

I ran downstairs to ask Mom for permission. I had to wait for several minutes because she and Mrs. Deets were in the middle of a conversation.

When she finally saw me fidgeting in the doorway she asked what was up.

"Cynthia and I need to look something up on the Internet. We want to do some quick research on Naitaka."

"That's the creature you are helping Dr. Gough find, right?" Mom asked.

"Right."

"Okay, but no videos or music downloads, okay? Our connection out here isn't as good as at home and is too expensive to do that."

"I'll only browse websites, Mom."

"You will let them do that alone?" Mrs. Deets asked looking worried.

Mom smiled at her. "Not to worry. I have web filters enabled on my laptop. Nothing will come up that I don't want them to see."

"Well...all right then."

"Run along, Mik," Mom said. "We ladies would like a bit more time to visit."

"Thanks, Mom," I said. I ran back up the stairs to where Cynthia waited.

"We have permission. Just no videos."

Cynthia nodded and I plunked down in front of Mom's laptop, plugging in search phrases Cynthia fed me. We tried all sorts of things: *hiding places at Lake Osowegol, hidden places at Lake Osowegol*. We used the word *cave* and *grotto*. We even tried searching for Naitaka.

Lots of information came up, but nothing that might tell us where a lake monster would be able to hide.

I lay down on the bed and stared at the ceiling. "Now what do we do? We can't hide the whole river where its egg is."

Cynthia lay on the bed beside me. "I don't know, Mik. Maybe we don't need to hide the creature. It's been in the lake for a long time, right?"

"Longer than people have been here according to the Guardian," I said.

"Then, maybe it already has some hiding spots. Maybe we don't need to find one for it."

That made sense. "But, what if Naitaka doesn't know it has to hide?"

"I guess we have to make it know," Cynthia said. I felt a flash of fear from her as she said it.

"If you don't want to go near it again, I will understand," I said.

"I'm okay," she said. "I'm not afraid to go with you."

I knew that wasn't completely true, but I didn't want to call her on her small fib. "Thanks, Cynthia. Having you with me makes me feel a whole lot better."

"But, let's not go back there quite yet," Cynthia said. "We should search a few more of the rivers and streams first. Maybe Naitaka has eggs down more than one. Besides, it would be suspicious if we kept going to the same place." Cynthia was trying hard to convince me that her only reasons didn't involve fear of Naitaka. I let it go.

"Okay, where do you want to go next?"

ΩΩΩ

We spent the next three days searching other steams, small rivers and swampy areas. I occasionally felt Naitaka out on the lake, but we never saw the creature. I could tell Cynthia wasn't bothered at all by not seeing it.

Each time we went out, we were careful to take pictures of the search areas, call in to Heidi regularly and appear to be doing our jobs.

On the fourth day we paddled back to Dr. Gough's camp to get a fresh memory card and batteries for our camera and just check in. We left Krypto behind because we expected a very short trip.

"We got rid of the pictures, right?" I asked for, probably the eighth time as we neared the pier. I was careful to keep my voice down because sound carried across the water.

"For the last time, yes!" Cynthia said. "Now stop worrying."

We beached the canoe and pulled it up on shore. Heidi came running down from the main tent as we secured everything on the beach.

"Hi, guys! How are you doing?"

As always, Heidi's enthusiasm was almost enough to mentally knock me over.

"We're great, Heidi, how are you?" Cynthia said. Cynthia's mood had lifted as soon as she heard Heidi's voice.

"I'm glad to have you here," she said. "It's nice to have company around camp for a change." She lowered her voice. "Dr. Gough, Charlie and Max spend most days out on the water so it's quiet here which is good. It does get a little boring though."

"I can believe it," I said. I changed the subject then. It was time to do a little digging. "Has Dr. Gough had any luck so far?"

"No, nothing definitive. A couple interesting sonar readings, but that's about it." Heidi smiled at me then. "And I've got to tell you two how much help you are. With our small team it would be really hard to cover the lake and all the tributaries too. Having you guys helping with those has taken a lot of stress off Dr. Gough." She sighed. "He works so hard, he deserves to find something to validate his research. If he fails this time, I don't know what he'll do."

That shook me and from the emotional echo from Cynthia, it bothered her too. I really liked Dr. Gough. Idolized him, if I were to be honest with myself. I had made a promise to him that I could no longer keep and it was really hard to hold onto the lie.

But I knew we had to protect Naitaka. Even from someone as well-intentioned as Dr. Gough.

"Uh, yeah. Thanks. We hope he finds the creature too," Cynthia said. I nodded vigorously, not quite sure what to add.

"By the way, guys. I had a question for you," Heidi said.

Alarm bells went off in my mind, but I managed to keep my face calm. "A question? What's that?"

"That first stream you went down. How far did you go?"

"All the way to the end. Why do you ask?" I said.

"To the end? So it didn't continue on into the hills?" Heidi asked.

"No, it stopped in a big pond." I was trying to figure out where her questions were going and not say anything that might give Naitaka or its egg away. I could feel Cynthia silently getting more and more afraid, probably that I would say something.

"Aha! I thought so!"

"Huh? I don't understand."

Heidi laughed. "Well, based on the maps we have, I surmised the water in the pond must be coming from underground sources. Maybe an entire underground river system. It would certainly explain the flow of water coming from nowhere."

"Oh, I see what you mean," I said. As I spoke I had an *aha* moment. If there *were* underground rivers, that could very well be where Naitaka dove when we left.

Then Heidi said something that sent a chill down my spine. "I can't wait to see the pictures from that pond. Maybe they will give an indication of where the underground source is coming in."

"Maybe," I said, with a little half laugh that I really didn't feel. "But, we didn't take a lot of pictures when we were down there. You might not see anything."

"I'll let you know if I find anything," Heidi said.

Cynthia, who was standing slightly behind Heidi, motioned toward the canoe with her head. "We should probably get back to work now. See what there is to be found."

"Oh. Right!" I said. "Thank you for everything, Heidi. We'll check in when we get to the next search point."

She smiled. "Sounds good, guys. Talk to you soon." She turned then and began to make her way back to the main tents.

"Come on, Mik. Time is wasting."

I followed Cynthia back to our canoe.

We didn't speak again until we were well away from the camp.

"Mik, I feel terrible about what we are doing. Maybe we should tell the doctor what we found and try to convince him not to turn Naitaka into a research project."

"I feel bad too, Cynthia, but telling him won't help. I read about his trip to Scotland. The locals tried to get him to stop but he wouldn't. He wasn't mean or cruel about it either. He just refused to leave. Now I understand why they let Nessie loose. It was that or have their version of Naitaka go to a lab somewhere."

We paddled in silence for several minutes then:"Mik?"

"Yes?"

"I'm worried. What if Heidi finds something in our pictures we didn't delete?"

"I was thinking that too," I admitted.

"I have a really bad feeling."

"Me too. So what do we do?"

"I think we need to go back to the pond. Today, if possible. We need to check that egg and try to send Naitaka away," Cynthia said, sounding and feeling more determined than I had ever heard or felt. "If nothing comes of the pictures, great. But, if Heidi *does* find something, wouldn't it be better if Naitaka were already gone?"

Ω Ω Ω

We were both covered in sweat when we arrived at the pond. I had felt the presence of Naitaka long before we arrived. I chose not to say anything to Cynthia because I knew she was still afraid of the creature, despite wanting to save it.

We paddled directly to the beach and I kept an eye out.

"Do you see anything?" I called up to Cynthia just before the canoe skidded onto the sand.

"There are a lot of tracks on the sand," Cynthia said. "The mound looks pretty messed up too." She pulled the canoe up onto the beach so I could climb out. We quickly pulled it further up onto the sand and ran over to check the mound.

All that was left were shards of the egg. We both knelt in the sand to get a better look.

Cynthia lifted the largest piece of shell for me to see. "Do you think the baby hatched?"

I shrugged. "I don't see any blood or body parts. I hope that means nothing got to the egg."

Cynthia's face scrunched up at that. "Eww! Gross, Mik."

"Sorry. Just telling you what I think," I said. I was about to say more, but I felt the presence of Naitaka really loom close then. Not an angry creature. Not even especially curious. Just...there. "Don't turn around Cynthia, but I think Naitaka is here right now."

Of course, what does everyone do when you say, *Don't look,* or *Don't turn around?* Naturally, they do exactly what you said *not* to do.

Cynthia turned. She let out a little squeak and her fear spiked.

I followed her example and turned around. Naitaka watched us from the edge of the water. A much smaller version of the creature sat next to our canoe.

"Hello, Naitaka," I said, hoping, but not expecting it to understand me. "There are scientists trying to find you. If they catch you, they will put you into an aquarium. You and your baby. You don't want that." As I spoke I tried the same trick I had used with the raccoons. Instead of a bear, I used faceless men with nets. I tried to show them catching Naitaka and dragging it off.

Naitaka continued to watch me from the water. The only indication I had that it was listening and perhaps getting my message was when it cocked it head at me.

"I can see the images you are projecting, Mik. Keep doing it," Cynthia whispered behind me.

I jumped a little, but kept going. "You must take your baby and hide. Maybe for a long time, Naitaka." I modified the images I was sending to show the creature going under the water and swimming down a long tunnel. I was really grasping now. After all, how do you give a message of hide and danger to a creature that may not even know the meaning of the words?

That's when Naitaka surprised me. It was something wholly unexpected. The creature sent back feelings of trust and friendship. It leaned toward Cynthia and me and stared at us for several moments, our images reflected back at us in its deep black eyes. Naitaka nudged me then, very gently, just like it had nudged its own egg several days before.

Then it drew back, turned and dove into the water. The baby followed its mother without hesitation. I reached out with my mind and felt their presence move away and then down and then…and then they were gone.

"Have they left?" Cynthia asked.

I could only nod. The creature's final emotions and gesture were of friendship. We hadn't even really spent any time with it, but somehow it understood we were trying to help it.

All I could think was *wow!* But instead I said, "Let's go home."

Chapter 31

I was watering the grass, waiting for Cynthia, when Dr. Gough came to the cabin. It was a couple days after Cynthia and I sent Naitaka away.

I went down to the pier to meet him.

I knew right away something was wrong. Dr. Gough's emotions clearly told me he was angry and disappointed at the same time.

"Hello, Dr. Gough," I said when he was in earshot."How are you today?"

His face didn't reveal the emotions I knew were just below the surface. "I'm confused, Mik. I was hoping you could clarify a few things for me."

"I'll try, Sir," I said. I had a sinking feeling I knew what this was about.

Dr. Gough handed me a piece of paper. It had a picture

that clearly showed the mound of sand and the egg on the beach. "I was hoping you could tell me about this picture."

"Where did you get that?" I asked.

"It was on the memory card you gave to Heidi a few days ago. It was actually a deleted picture that Heidi found on the card after doing some digital diagnostics. Apparently, there were pictures missing in the sequence you provided to her. She was just checking to see if they were corrupted or lost or whatever."

What could I tell this man whom I idolized? I suppose I could simply lie to him. Play dumb. But he deserved better than that.

I sighed. "We deleted those pictures, Dr. Gough."

I've got to give him credit. He didn't yell then, but remained calm. "May I ask why?"

"I knew if you saw them, you would capture Naitaka. You would take it away for study and something amazing would leave the world."

He shook his head and his emotions took on a sadness then. "I thought I could trust you, Mik. It turns out you are a liar just like the others were." He held out his hand. "My radio and camera, if you please."

"But, Dr. Gough—"

"We have nothing further to say to each other. We're done. Just bring me back my gear."

I nodded, feeling very numb. "Just a minute. I'll go get it for you."

I don't really remember much of what happened next. I know I gave him his equipment and he left. I was sitting on the porch, petting Krypto when Cynthia came.

"Hey, Mik. Ready to go back out searching?"

"There won't be any more searching, Cynthia. Dr. Gough

found the deleted pictures. He's already come by to get his equipment."

"Oh."

A lot can be said in a single word and Cynthia had just said a mouthful.

I shook my head. "We did the right thing, didn't we?"

Cynthia sat down beside me. "I think we did. Don't you?"

"I do. So why do I feel so bad?"

"You admired Dr. Gough; he was your hero. Maybe you feel like you betrayed him?"

I nodded. "I do. I absolutely feel like I betrayed him. I think it's even worse because of what he said when he left."

"What was that?"

"He I was a liar just like the others. I can only guess the others he meant were the people who let Nessie go."

"Mik!" Cynthia waited for me to look at her before speaking again. "Mik, has it ever occurred to you that the others thought just like we did? They didn't want something wonderful to be taken away for study. They wanted their creature to live free just like we do."

"I suppose."

"Then maybe we are right and Dr. Gough is wrong. Maybe he should think about what he is trying to do and follow a different path."

I thought about that. It made a lot of sense. It didn't erase the hurt, but it helped ease it. I gave Cynthia a hug. "I'm so glad you are my friend, Cynthia. I would be lost without you."

Ω Ω Ω

"Hey, Mik, how are you doing today?" Cynthia asked.

I had been sitting on the porch, scratching behind Krypto's ears and waiting for Cynthia to arrive. We had a day of exploring planned, in fact had been planning for a couple days. Mom even packed us a lunch.

I knew we weren't going exploring today.

"I was okay until you got here," I said.

Cynthia looked at me for several moments before she said anything. "Mik, I thought I asked you not to read my feelings."

I shook my head. "I didn't really have to try. You have been projecting since you first got into my range. What's the matter?"

Cynthia sighed and sat down beside me, staring out at the lake. "Father came home last night." She stopped talking like that should explain everything.

It didn't really tell me much at all. I waited for a few seconds before I spoke. "And?"

"And, it's the middle of the week."

I thought about that. "Um, you're going to have to be a little clearer than that. I'm not quite sure what that means."

She sighed again and turned to face me directly. "Father coming home in the middle of the week means his job in Cranberry Flats is done. It means it's time for my family to go home."

"Go home?" I tried to wrap my head around that. "Go home?" I said it with a slightly different emphasis on the word to see if the sentence's meaning would change. It didn't.

"But you can't go home now!" I said. "The summer isn't over yet. We still have exploring to do and swimming and canoeing...." I stopped speaking when I realized I was rambling.

Krypto sat up and stared at me, whining just a little.

"Mik, you're projecting again," Cynthia said softly. She sniffed and scrubbed at her eyes. "I don't want to leave yet either."

"It's just...." I searched for the right words to say. Nothing came to mind so I sat and shook my head.

"I know, Mik. I tried to talk Mother and Father into staying longer, but they said we couldn't. Father must get onto his next job and that is back home." Cynthia's feelings were rapidly changing from sadness to guilt to misery and back again.

I straightened up. "I'm sorry, Cynthia. I don't mean to make you feel bad. I just thought we would have the whole summer to do stuff together. We still don't know if Naitaka or her baby will be coming back." I looked at her. I finally noticed her red-rimmed eyes and red nose.

I suddenly felt very selfish.

"But we can stay in touch with each other, right?" I asked, trying to change the subject. Dwelling on what we couldn't change would only make it harder on Cynthia. Harder on me too, if I wanted to admit it.

Cynthia brightened at that and I felt her first feelings of hope and happiness. "You would want to stay in touch with me?"

"Of course! Why wouldn't I?" I asked, confused a little by her surprise.

She shrugged. "I just wondered if you would want to stay friends, what with me being a girl and all."

That made no sense to me. "Cynthia, you are one of my best friends. Because of you, this summer has been a lot of fun. You have to admit, we've done some pretty amazing things together."

She smiled then. "I know that, silly! But I've known plenty of boys who want nothing to do with a girl. I wondered if we were only hanging out because we're the only two kids around here."

"Nope," I said. "That might have been the case when I first met you, but now I spend time with you because you are a really cool person." I pointed at my dog. "And Krypto here likes you too and he's a pretty fussy guy about people."

At the mention of his name, Krypto's tail began to wag. He went over to Cynthia and gave her a slobbery dog kiss.

Cynthia giggled. "Enough, Krypto. I love you too!" She gently pushed his probing nose out of her face.

"When will you be leaving?"

"This weekend. Sunday, I think. We have packing to do and Mother and Father wanted to say goodbye to your parents properly." She held up an envelope. "Part of the reason I'm here is to deliver this invitation to your mom."

"Are you able to go exploring today?" I asked.

Cynthia's smile was sad. "I'm afraid not, Mik. Mother wants me back at the cabin to help pack and cleanup. There's a lot to do and not very much time to do it."

I nodded. "I understand." I stood up. "Do you think your parents would mind if I came over today to help you pack? I seem to have some time available in my schedule."

"You mean it?" Cynthia jumped to her feet and gave me a huge hug. "I know they wouldn't mind."

"Then, let's get that invitation into the house and I'll tell Mom where I'm going to be today."

Epilogue

After my adventures with Cynthia, the rest of the summer was downright boring. I spent most of it helping Mom around the cabin and going for walks with Krypto. It was a relief when we finally left the lake.

The first thing I did when we were home, after helping unload the truck that is, was go for a walk around town with Krypto.

I'd worried being away from town left Cranberry Flats unprotected. What I saw confirmed that. Graffiti coated many of the walls, fences and buildings. Over and over I saw the same images. There were names, pictures and references to the *Big Boss. The Big Boss owns this...the Big Boss is coming to get you.*

I had thought I'd gotten rid of the Big Boss when I chased his minions out of town the first time I encountered them. I had to chuckle when I remembered how Krypto and I had pelted those men, one of whom was dressed like a large

246

glowing turkey, into submission with fresh cow pies. They had begged to be arrested when we were finished.

I thought back to my encounter with the graffiti gang before we left town. They had talked about being paid. I wondered if someone, maybe this Big Boss, was paying people to deface my town. And if he was, why? Graffiti never made sense to me – damaging other people's property by defacing and damaging it didn't do anyone any good.

That made me angry.

The Big Boss and the people who worked for him obviously thought my town was theirs to mess up.

I wasn't about to let that happen.

I was pretty sure I wouldn't find the rats that were decorating my town during the day. Their kind usually hides from prying eyes. I walked around, noting all the graffiti and then I went home to prepare.

The first time I went after the graffiti artists I hadn't known what I was up against. I had been in too much of a hurry to make sure I was ready.

I lost my cape and barely escaped that time.

I was going to be ready now *and* I had honed my new power. I had better control of sensing people's emotions and my time using my ability to scare away the raccoons and get Naitaka to leave gave me new confidence. It was time for the showdown.

Krypto and I spent the day out at the treehouse. I gathered fresh cow pies and did what I could to ready my costume and other weapons. Then, I used my powers to try moving the steers around for practise.

When Mom tucked me into bed, I knew I was ready. As wonderful as it was to finally be sleeping in my own bed in my own house again, I had to deal with the troublemakers first.

I waited until Mom and Dad were asleep before I carried out my plan. I gave Krypto the mental command to meet me outside. I climbed out my bedroom window onto the porch and shimmied down the tree beside it to the ground.

Krypto and I ran all the way to the treehouse to get equipped.

Just like the last time, I took my listening ear. The difference this time was, I had fresh batteries in the device. It should work properly.

Costumed and with weapons and gadgets ready, Krypto and I went on patrol.

We had been out for almost an hour and I was beginning to think we wouldn't have any luck finding our quarry. That's when I sensed the emotional presence of some people down a very dark alley. Three people to be exact. The same number that I had run into all those weeks ago.

But, that wasn't enough evidence to convict anyone of wrongdoing. So I trained the listening ear onto the alley to try and determine what, if anything was going on.

I clearly heard the telltale sound of a spray bottle being used.

Bingo.

I used my mind to reach out to the alley and felt the three distinct personalities at work. I couldn't be sure – it had been a few months – but it felt like the same people as before.

I set down the backpack and pulled out the first of my weapons from a plastic grocery bag I had been carrying. Crusty on the outside, gooey in the middle, cow pies. I hefted it experimentally in my hand to judge its weight.

This was nothing like the cow pies I had tried in the spring. It wasn't dried out and desiccated. This one was only a few days old.

I let it fly.

The yell of anger told me clearly I had scored a direct hit. My opponents wasted no time and came running out of the alley.

I didn't bother to hide. I threw the next cow pie as they came out of the alley, hitting the first one square in the chest.

The light was a lot better to night; the moon was almost full and the alley was near a streetlight. I had no trouble seeing the red cape worn by one of the three goons.

My red cape.

They turned toward me, yelling and threatening. I was ready. I projected the image of a large snake at the one wearing my cape.

She screamed, tearing at the cape. "Get it off! *Get it off!*"

The two ahead of her turned to see what was going on. I launched another cow pie, hitting the closest guy in the back. He turned, dripping manure from both sides.

"I don't know who you are, but I'm going to rip your head off," he threatened.

That's when I projected the image and feeling of ants scrambling over and into his clothing. He started slapping at his clothes and then dropped to the ground, rolling and shrieking.

By this time, the girl had the cape off and was backing away from it in horror. Her accomplice, who had helped her to pull it off, watched his friends in confusion. The third had stopped rolling and had ripped off most of his clothing.

I'm not quite sure what pushed them over the edge but, one moment they were there, and the next they were running away as hard as they could.

I considered chasing them, but I knew that would be foolish. Sure, I might find out where they lived or where their hideout was, but I might also find myself in a lot of trouble if they turned on me.

No, the smart thing to do would be to take the victory and be done for the night.

Krypto and I collected my cape and headed for home.

It was a small victory, but it *was* a victory. I knew I would face them again but just being back, I felt better. More complete. Especially with my new power under better control.

I considered my summer of exile from town and realized just how important it had been. It had given me the chance to hone and learn to use my powers. It had given me the chance to save a legendary creature. It had given me new confidence in myself and in my abilities.

Most importantly, it had given me the chance to make a new friend.

That felt good right up until I remembered my decisions had also alienated someone I really respected.

Why did the important decisions so often carry such consequences? I thought about the Spider-man movie for the first time in months, remembering what Uncle Ben had said to Peter Parker. "With great power comes great responsibility."

I wasn't quite sure I wanted the responsibility but, if not me then who? I knew the answer to that question. It had to be me. I would protect my town, my family and my friends. That was my fate as a super hero.

I wondered for the briefest of moments; what would be my next battle? What would be my next adventure? Would I ever see Cynthia again? They were all questions that I had no answers to. But that was all right. I had friends and a family that loved me. I had my power and I was Mik Murdoch, Boy Superhero.

About the Author

Michell Plested has been reading science fiction and fantasy since he was six years old and writing for almost as long. He is an author, blogger and podcaster living in Calgary, Alberta, Canada. He writes in multiple genres spending most of his time with science fiction, fantasy and YA adventure.

He is the host of the writing podcast *Get Published,* a 2009 Parsec Finalist and the Science Fiction Comedy podcast *GalaxyBillies* which has been called "Hitchiker's Guide to the Galaxy meets Beverley Hillbillies" by his listeners.

His first novel, *Mik Murdoch: Boy Superhero,* was shortlisted for the 2013 Prix Aurora, Best YA Novel.

Books by Five Rivers

NON-FICTION

Al Capone: Chicago's King of Crime, by Nate Hendley

Crystal Death: North America's Most Dangerous Drug, by Nate Hendley

Dutch Schultz: Brazen Beer Baron of New York, by Nate Hendley

John Lennon: Music, Myth and Madness, by Nate Hendley

Motivate to Create: a guide for writers, by Nate Hendley

Stephen Truscott, Decades of Injustice by Nate Hendley

Shakespeare for Slackers: Romeo and Juliet, by Aaron Kite, Audrey Evans and Jade Brooke

The Organic Home Gardener, by Patrick Lima and John Scanlan

Elephant's Breath & London Smoke: historic colour names, definitions & uses, Deb Salisbury, editor

Stonehouse Cooks, by Lorina Stephens

Shakespeare for Readers' Theatre: Hamlet, Romeo & Juliet, Midsummer Night's Dream, by John Poulson

FICTION

Black Wine, by Candas Jane Dorsey

88, by M.E. Fletcher

Immunity to Strange Tales, by Susan J. Forest

The Legend of Sarah, by Leslie Gadallah

Growing Up Bronx, by H.A. Hargreaves

North by 2000+, a collection of short, speculative fiction, by H.A. Hargreaves

A Subtle Thing, Alicia Hendley

Downshift, a Sid Rafferty Thriller, by Matt Hughes

Old Growth, a Sid Rafferty Thriller by Matt Hughes

The Tattooed Witch, by Susan MacGregor

The Tattooed Seer, by Susan MacGregor

Kingmaker's Sword, Book 1: Rune Blades of Celi, by Ann Marston

Western King, Book 2: The Rune Blades of Celi, by Ann Marston

Broken Blade, Book 3: The Rune Blades of Celi, by Ann Marston

Cloudbearer's Shadow, Book 4: The Rune Blades of Celi, by Ann Marston

King of Shadows, Book 5: The Rune Blades of Celi, by Ann Marston

Indigo Time, by Sally McBride

Wasps at the Speed of Sound, by Derryl Murphy

A Method to Madness: A Guide to the Super Evil, edited by Michell Plested and Jeffery A. Hite

A Quiet Place, by J.W. Schnarr

Things Falling Apart, by J.W. Schnarr

And the Angels Sang: a collection of short speculative fiction, by Lorina Stephens

From Mountains of Ice, by Lorina Stephens

Memories, Mother and a Christmas Addiction, by Lorina Stephens

Shadow Song, by Lorina Stephens

YA FICTION

My Life as a Troll, by Susan Bohnet

The Runner and the Wizard, by Dave Duncan

The Runner and the Saint, by Dave Duncan

The Runner and the Kelpie, by Dave Duncan

A Touch of Poison, by Aaron Kite

Out of Time, by D.G. Laderoute

Mik Murdoch: Boy-Superhero, by Michell Plested

Mik Murdoch: The Power Within, by Michell Plested

Type, by Alicia Hendley

FICTION COMING SOON

Cat's Pawn, by Leslie Gadallah

Cat's Gambit, by Leslie Gadallah

Revenant, by Aaron Kite

The Tattooed Rose, by Susan MacGregor

Sword and Shadow, Book 6: The Rune Blades of Celi, by Ann Marston

Bane's Choice, Book 7: The Rune Blades of Celi, by Ann Marston

A Still and Bitter Grave, by Ann Marston

Diamonds in Black Sand, by Ann Marston

YA FICTION COMING SOON

Type2, by Alicia Hendley

The Journals of Vincent Tucat: Two Cats, Book 1, by Aaron Kite

The Journals of Vincent Tucat: Jade Mouse, Book 2, by Aaron Kite

The Journals of Vincent Tucat: Ten Arrows, Book 3, by Aaron Kite

NON-FICTION COMING SOON

Annotated Henry Butte's Dry Dinner, by Michelle Enzinas

King Kwong, by Paula Johanson

Shakespeare for Slackers: Hamlet, by Aaron Kite and Audrey Evans

Shakespeare for Slackers: Macbeth, by Aaron Kite and Audrey Evans

Shakespeare for Reader's Theatre, Book 2: Shakespeare's Greatest Villains, The Merry Wives of Windsor; Othello, the Moor of Venice; Richard III; King Lear, by John Poulsen

YA NON-FICTION COMING SOON

The Prime Ministers of Canada Series:

Sir John A. Macdonald

Alexander Mackenzie

Sir John Abbott

Sir John Thompson

Sir Mackenzie Bowell

Sir Charles Tupper

Sir Wilfred Laurier

Sir Robert Borden

Arthur Meighen

William Lyon Mackenzie King

R. B. Bennett

Louis St. Laurent

John Diefenbaker

Lester B. Pearson

Pierre Trudeau

Joe Clark

John Turner

Brian Mulroney

Kim Campbell

Jean Chretien

Paul Martin

WWW.FIVERIVERSPUBLISHING.C

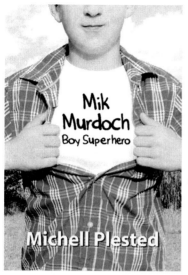

Mik Murdoch, Boy Superhero
by Michell Plested

ISBN 9781927400111 $23.99

eISBN 9781927400128 $4.99

Trade Paperback 6 x 9

226 pages

August 1, 2012

A delightful and truly Canadian tale of a 9 year old boy's quest to protect his prairie town of Cranberry Flats, and in his search to acquire super-powers finds the most awesome power of all lies within his own inherent integrity

Shortlisted for the 2013 Prix Aurora, Best YA Novel.

Out of Time
by D.G. Laderoute

ISBN 9781927400371 $23.99

eISBN 9781927400388 $4.99

Trade Paperback 6 x 9

294 pages

November 1, 2013

For Riley Corbeau, moving to a small town on Superior's north shore was an opportunity for his family to find a new beginning after the death of his mother. For Gathering Cloud, living on Kitche Gumi's shore now meant it was time seek a vision and become a man. There on a beach of this legendary lake, two boys meet across time and impossibilities, brought together to face an ancient evil from Anishnabe folklore, and in doing so forge a friendship that defies time

Shortlisted for the 2014 Prix Aurora, Best YA Novel.

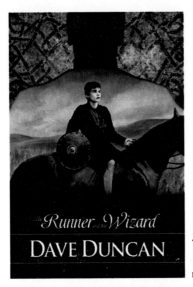

The Runner and the Wizard

by Dave Duncan

ISBN 9781927400395 $11.99

eISBN 9781927400401 $4.99

Trade Paperback 6 x 9

100 pages

October 1, 2013

Young Ivor dreams of being a swordsman like his nine older brothers, but until he can grow a beard he's limited to being a runner, carrying messages for their lord, Thane Carrak. That's usually boring, but this time Carrak has sent him on a long journey to summon the mysterious Rorie of Ytter. Rorie is reputed to be a wizard—or an outlaw, or maybe a saint—but the truth is far stranger, and Ivor suddenly finds himself caught up in a twisted magical intrigue that threatens Thane Carrak and could leave Ivor himself very dead.

The Runner and the Saint

by Dave Duncan

ISBN 9781927400531 $11.99

eISBN 9781927400548 $4.99

Trade Paperback 6 x 9

114 pages

March 1, 2014

Earl Malcolm has reason to fear the ferocious Northmen raiders of the Western Isles are going to attack the land of Alba, so he sends Ivor on a desperate mission with a chest of silver to buy them off. But the situation Ivor finds when he reaches the Wolf's Lair is even worse than he was led to expect. Only a miracle can save him now

A Touch of Poison

by Aaron Kite

ISBN 9781927400593 $19.99

eISBN 9781927400609 $4.99

Trade Paperback 6 x 9

234 pages

August 1, 2014

Gwenwyn, who is the most miserable princess ever, and for good reason. Merely brushing up against her or touching her exposed skin is enough to cause painful burns, or worse. And if that wasn't enough, she's just discovered the singular reason for her existence - to act as the king's secret assassin, murdering neighboring princes with nothing more than a simple kiss.

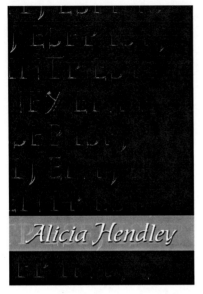

Type
By Alicia Hendley
ISBN 9781927400296 $31.99
eISBN 9781927400302
Trade Paperback 6 x 9
314 pages
June 1, 2013

After the fallout from the Social Media Era, when rates of divorce, crime, and mental illness were sky-rocketing, civilization was at its breaking point. As a result, prominent psychologists from around the globe gathered together to try to regain social order through scientific means.

Their solution? Widespread implementation of Myers-Briggs personality typing, with each citizen assessed at the age of twelve and then sent to one of sixteen Home Schools in order to receive the appropriate education for their Type and aided in choosing a suitable occupation and life partner.

North American society becomes structured around the tenets of Typology, with governments replaced by The Association of Psychologists. With social order seemingly regained, what could go possibly wrong?

Mik Murdoch

The Power Within

Contest

So, here's the deal. Get yourself a copy of *Mik Murdoch: The Power Within* as soon as you're able. Read it. All of it. And while you're doing that remember all your best scouting lessons, because you're going to need them. In fact, mapping skills is what you're going to need. Why? Because there are coordinates you're going to need, and once you find them you have to pinpoint the exact location for us, email us at mik@5rivers.org what you've found with your super-mapping powers. If you're the first, you'll win a free digital copy of D.G. Laderoute's fabulous YA fantasy, *Out of Time*.

CPSIA information can be obtained at www.ICGtesting.com
Printed in the USA
LVOW07s0519081014

407698LV00003B/13/P